I0762794

BLOODY GOLD

Center Point
Large Print

Also by Peter Dawson and available from Center Point Large Print:

The Stirrup Brand
Dark Riders of Doom

BLOODY GOLD

PETER DAWSON

Center Point Large Print
Thorndike, Maine

This Center Point Large Print edition
is published in the year 2026 by arrangement with
Golden West Inc.

The text of this Large Print edition is unabridged.
In other aspects, this book may vary
from the original edition.
Printed in the United States of America
on permanent paper sourced using
environmentally responsible foresting methods.
Set in 16-point Times New Roman type.

ISBN: 979-8-89164-897-5

The Library of Congress has cataloged this record
under Library of Congress Control Number: 2026932469

BLOODY GOLD

1

Johnny Terrell rode the stronger horse because he was a big man. It took a horse with a good back to carry him. He was outsized for sure, with heavy shoulders and long arms and legs ending in huge hands and feet. When Johnny made a fist, men looked at it and shuddered. His face was common enough yet complicated by pale blue eyes that appeared childish. He was young, true, but men who took him to be childish made a fatal mistake.

Toomey rode the small horse because he did not weigh more than one hundred and twenty pounds in wet boots. He was small, but he could do a twelve-hour day's work with the best and still have enough left over for his woman. He was as old as Johnny was young, which is to say neither man was too old nor too young. They had been riding together for many days, and they had long since stopped looking around over the shoulder. No one was on their back trail.

Toomey reined suddenly for no reason, and his horse swung its head and looked at him reprovingly. It was hard to get started again once the rhythm of the stride had been broken, and Toomey's horse was bone tired.

"How far?" asked Toomey.

He sounded more mad than discouraged.

Johnny Terrell reined in and deliberately removed his hat and mopped his brow before answering. He stared west then, shielding his eyes with his hand against the glare of the desert.

"Two, three days, maybe," said Johnny.

"God," said Toomey.

There were not any landmarks that Toomey could see. The earth was bare, and the only difference in it was the size of one pebble from another. The horses' hoofs suffered from the heat of the sand, and they were both going lame. The country was cut by dry washes in every direction. There was no vegetation to hold the water, and the soil had been washed clean to gravel. They had been working south and west for four days, and the further they went, the worse the terrain had become. Now they sat their horses on a ridge between two dry washes, and as far as Toomey could see, the desert stretched, endless and forbidding. Toomey spat.

"I've never been nowhere in my life I could see so much land all at once," said Toomey, "with so little in it to see."

"Yonder's the mountain," said Johnny.

Toomey squinted his eyes and stared west, but he could not make it out at first. The awesome distances visible in this land played tricks on the eyes. If the eye focused just short or long of an object, it might as well not exist. A man would not see it. Toomey let his eyes do their own adjusting, and after a moment, he thought he saw a vague difference on the horizon, an off-white shade against the skyline.

"I'm used to mountains that are green," said Toomey. "Light green for foothills, and as the ridges grow higher and farther away, they become darker until the highest and farthest away is purple."

"No trees on this one," said Johnny. "No rain falls on this side, but on the opposite slope the trees grow tall."

"I don't think I can take three more days."

"Not even for gold?"

"Don't count on it until it's in your hand," said Toomey.

Johnny studied Toomey.

"I wouldn't have shown you the way if you hadn't sworn it was there," said Johnny. "And easy to get at."

"It's there. I'm just tired. Don't pay me any mind. I'm too wrung out to think."

"You'll get drier before we hit the mountain and start climbing. The last water hole is just ahead. Tomorrow and the next day are dry runs. All the water we carry will be for the horses."

"Jesus God," said Toomey. "It beats me how anything can live out here. I think you're kidding about Indians. Not even an Indian would live here."

"There are Indians," said Johnny. "We haven't seen any, but that's not important. They haven't seen us, that's the point. That's why you still have your hair. Talk about dry, they'd stake you down spread-eagle under the sun and tan you like a deer hide. That's dry!"

They rode on, Toomey sticking close to Johnny. This was all new to him. He had never been away from the mines of Georgia until this trip. He had started in coal mines at ten years of age and moved on to small hard-rock gold mines, and he knew everything there was to know about tunneling and milling. He knew coal and gold, and Johnny Terrell knew the desert. There was no better man with horses than Johnny, and there were very few men faster with a handgun or their fists. Toomey was an expert at his trade and had his own honest pride, but he was smart enough to do the following when he played another man's game.

In time, they topped a rise and sat their horses, looking down on a shallow swale containing the water hole. A mud wallow was all it turned out to be. Johnny did not ride down but held his horse under tight rein. The horse smelled moisture and was crazy to get at it.

Dry grass grew here and a few scrub trees with thin limbs as brittle and bare as the legs of beetles. Instead of the expectation of refreshment, Toomey felt the excitement of fear grip at his stomach. He held his breath. There was a sense of waiting in the silence of the desert.

"Indians?" asked Toomey.

"Don't know yet," said Johnny.

His voice was so quiet that it scared Toomey more than the unknown danger, and Toomey started when a flock of buzzards rose up from the other side of the swale, their flight erratic on awkward wings.

Johnny rode around the swale with Toomey right behind, and they found the carrion birds' prey, a dead horse. A little further away lay a man, or his bones at least, picked clean by the buzzards.

"Not a day old," said Johnny.

The bones were not bleached under the sun, and they could see black, raw shreds of meat at the ankles inside the high-topped boots where the buzzards had not got at it. They rode back to the lip of the water hole.

"Stay here and keep your eyes open," said Johnny.

He dismounted and handed Toomey the reins and went down to the water hole and squatted on his heels. He scooped away a place for water to gather and rested on his haunches while he waited for water to seep in and make a pool. He tasted the water with his lips but did not swallow, then he spat viciously and stood up, wiping his hands on his jeans. He studied the ground in the swale carefully, then climbed to the lip and walked all around it, examining the earth. He stopped once and bent down to look at something, and when he came back to the horses, his usually untroubled face wore a frown.

"What's wrong?" asked Toomey.

"Poisoned," said Johnny.

"Can't drink it? Not at all?"

"He did," said Johnny, indicating the dead man.

"Poisoned how?"

"I don't know," said Johnny. "There've been a lot of horses here, shod horses, not Indian. Not cavalry either. The water hole's been blown out with black powder. Maybe they did it to protect people. Maybe they did it to close off the water. When you blast a hole out here, you usually ruin it."

"Why would anybody do that?"

"I don't know."

"What are we going to do?" asked Toomey.

"Wait for dark."

"These horses can't go on without water."

"Moving by night will save them some. How much water you got left?"

Toomey held up his two-gallon canteen and shook it, and it was almost empty.

"Doesn't matter," said Johnny. "I've got enough in mine to get us through."

"And the horses?" asked Toomey.

Johnny did not answer. He was already unsaddling.

Toomey got down and followed Johnny's example, thankful that Johnny had not said any more. Toomey had taken frequent drinks from his canteen, and the more he had sipped, the more he had thirsted, until he had not been able to keep from taking a long, full, Adam's-apple-bobbing drink. Even that had not helped. Johnny had never more than wet his lips from his own canteen, and he had most of his water left.

They hobbled the horses and tied them to a heavy rock so they would not go to the swale, and Toomey guarded them while Johnny piled stones on the body of the dead man. The rocks were so hot under the sun that they burned the flesh, and Johnny had to wear his gloves to get the job done. When he returned, he was carrying what was left of the man's possessions. The beaks of the carrion birds were so strong and sharp that there was little left to identify.

"Canteen, possible sack with chow," said Johnny. "Slicker, bedroll, hat. He wasn't a cowboy."

"How can you tell?" asked Toomey.

"His boots. They're low-heeled."

"Heavy-toed and run over. Soles wore out," added Toomey. "I noticed that. He was a miner. Probably came from the mines up on the mountain. Did he have a poke?"

"Didn't find one."

"No saddlebags?"

"Nope."

"He might have had gold on him. You're not holding out on me?"

Johnny looked square at Toomey.

"I'm sorry," said Toomey. "I didn't mean to doubt you."

"You didn't?"

"I told you I was sorry. Hell, if he was from the mines why'd he come this way? A man with nothing to hide would go north, around the desert, by way of the towns. He came here because he had to. Why? Because he was running. Why does a man run? Because he stole something. If he stole something, it's still on him, because we're the first ones to come by."

"Go look for yourself," said Johnny.

"Aren't you interested?"

"You're awful sure there's something to find."

"I'm using my head. I never knew a miner that didn't always have a little gold put by, even if it was only a few specimens. How long would it take him to die?"

"He'd know something was wrong the first gulp, but he must have been too thirsty to stop. He hadn't had a drink of fresh water for two days and nights. If he got a bellyful, he probably died in two, three hours."

"All right, he knew he was sick, too sick to get back on his horse and move on. He died right here. Now, he didn't have a lot of gold, or he'd have a pack animal to carry it. Gold's heavy. He didn't have saddlebags, or at least we haven't found them. He just had a little leather bag with drawstrings to hold it shut, and when he knew he wasn't going to make it, he scooped out a hole and buried his poke."

"That's a wild guess."

"I haven't been a miner all my life for nothing. You get gold fever, and it's worse than anything. Worse than the bottle, more nagging than women, more beautiful than dreams made of poppy. Even in death, a miner will think of his gold first, last, and amen."

"If it was me, I'd take out insurance," said Johnny, looking off toward the mound of stones. "I wouldn't give up. I'd never believe I wouldn't make it."

"What would you do?"

"I'd put my gun with the poke," said Johnny. "You never know who's going to find you, and when I reached for that poke, I'd want to come up with a gun. We never found his gun, and nobody would come this way without some kind of protection."

"Now you're getting the idea," said Toomey. "Let's find it."

"Go ahead. I'll watch the horses."

"Where'll I start?"

"He must have sat down to wait for dark just like us. He died sitting there. It's not ten yards from where he lies."

Toomey got up and went away, and he was back in fifteen minutes, carrying an old Colt Dragoon pistol and a soft leather bag about ten inches long. The bag hung heavy at the bottom, and Toomey tossed the pistol to Johnny, who caught it deftly and turned it over in his hands.

"What does that tell you?" asked Toomey.

"He wasn't a gunman," said Johnny.

He sighted down the barrel and spun the cylinder.

"Hasn't been rifled. Accurate to twenty yards at most. Weighs over four pounds. Too heavy to use quick."

"Now look at these," said Toomey.

He opened the drawstrings and poured gold nuggets into Johnny's open palm.

"What do they say to you?" asked Toomey.

"Where'd you find them?"

"You must have piled a hundred rocks on the corpse. They were under the one close rock you didn't turn over."

Toomey hesitated, his grizzled, unshaven face thoughtful.

"You knew that water was tainted before we saw the buzzards," stated Toomey.

"Not for sure. I just felt something."

"Something you can't explain? Something mysterious?"

"You get used to following instinct," said Johnny. "I don't consider my instinct mysterious.

The sign was all wrong. Animals had left the place alone. Their sign only came close and backed off. The wallow should have been churned to mud, but it wasn't. I got a bad feeling about it."

"So you tested it?"

"You test most everything out here."

"That man didn't," said Toomey.

"What are you getting at?"

"Gold tells me stories. It reveals its secrets to me just as your instinct does for you. That gold you're holding is high-grade."

"Valuable?"

"Oh, it'd assay a good thirty dollars to the ounce, but I don't mean that. It's stolen."

"How can you tell?"

"Those aren't natural nuggets, now, like you'd pan out of a stream. They've been melted down, smelted out of crushed ore. Our man probably worked for wages in a mine. When he ran across a piece of ore with a lot of pure gold visible in it, he took a quick look around to see if he was being watched, and then he hid it and took it home. That's high-grading. You only take high-grade ore."

"How'd he get it milled? Maybe he had his own little mine that played out, and this was all he got."

"A man wouldn't carry a mill around with him. He couldn't. He'd send his ore to a commercial mill that handled that for all the little independents. A sampler mill, it's called. He wouldn't get gold in return, anyway. They sample each ton or so of ore, and then they pay cash for the percentage of gold per ton. It's high-grade, Johnny. Back home, everybody does it.

"Every miner has his own little mill to refine high-grade. Kids grow up learning it at their daddy's knee. Owners pay starvation wages, and high-grade is considered a part of your pay, like totin' privileges."

"What happens if you get caught stealing?" asked Johnny.

"High-grading, please. Fired! No notice, no questions, and you just move over to the next mine until you get caught there. The managers don't care as long as you don't get caught. They believe a man will work harder if he's looking for some for himself."

"Don't you run out of places to work?"

"Eventually. Then you head west like me. But I've got ambition. There's no future in working for wages. I want my own mine someday."

"So they can high-grade from you?"

"I know all the tricks. Surprising how much gold you can hide in a bushy head of hair. Some men have special pockets sewn in their underwear. You can carry enough gold home in your mouth to feed a family for a month. I've known men to carry high-grade out in a tube inserted in their anus. Don't look disgusted. It's rent and food money. It pays for the kids' winter shoes. I'd make my men change clothes in a special room. I'd send their dinner down in company buckets, and when the men came out of the ground, they'd have to wash and change into their other clothes again. I'd pay a living wage. A man shouldn't be forced to steal."

Johnny handed the nuggets back, and they were both silent, both thinking the same thing. It had been a funny thing for Toomey to say. Here they were on the way to do some stealing, big stealing, and nobody was forcing them to it.

Toomey turned the poke upside down, holding the bottom of the bag in one hand, and the nuggets poured out into his open palm. He put the poke aside and weighed the nuggets in both hands until he had them evenly divided and held out half to Johnny.

Johnny took them.

"How much would this come to?" asked Johnny.

"Couple of hundred dollars," said Toomey.

"It weighs heavy," said Johnny. "How are we going to carry off a hundred thousand dollars' worth?"

"That's a problem."

"Maybe it's time you told me about it."

"Don't worry. It's all been worked out beforehand. I'm a careful man, Johnny."

"Not so careful," said Johnny. "I got the best of the bargain. Don't you want your share?"

He raised the old Dragoon pistol and pointed the muzzle right at Toomey, who looked at Johnny's face. Toomey could not read anything there, and he checked his breath. Johnny watched Toomey's face as he pulled the trigger.

Toomey was frozen. He was too surprised to react, and he just sat there with his mouth open while the hammer on the big gun fell. There was no explosion. The gun misfired, and Johnny smiled.

Toomey let the air out of his lungs all at once. He looked like he was going to faint.

"Why'd you do that?" he asked. "You could have killed me."

"Maybe," said Johnny.

"How could you be sure it wouldn't go off?"

Toomey almost shouted it.

"Center-five cartridges in a rim-fire gun," explained Johnny. "That man couldn't have used this gun if he'd wanted to."

"It was a fool thing to do."

"You're the fool."

"Why?"

Toomey was beginning to get mad now that he had his wind back.

"You held some gold out in the bottom of the poke when you turned it up. You held on to some with your hand," said Johnny.

Toomey tried to meet Johnny's gaze, but he could not and he reached down beside him and picked up the poke and turned it upside down again. Four more nuggets fell out.

"Just my share," said Johnny.

Toomey gave Johnny two more pieces of gold.

"It don't amount to fifty dollars," said Toomey, passing it off.

"That isn't the point. We're going after a hundred thousand, and here you are cheating me over fifty. I can't trust you."

"I'm sorry. I'm just naturally dishonest. I had a grandpappy who put it this way: 'Honesty may be the best policy, but a man owes it to himself to try everything else first.' Now that you've caught me out, I won't try and cheat you again."

"I had a grandpappy too," said Johnny. "He used to say, 'You don't know a man entirely until you divide an inheritance with him.' I'll take you to the mountain, but when we get there, you're on your own."

"I need you, Johnny. I can't do it alone. There's others in on it, and I need someone on my side."

Johnny shook his head. He had made up his mind.

"You'll change," said Toomey. "A poor man can't pass up a hundred thousand when it's so easy to get. A poor man doesn't come by more than one chance like this in a lifetime."

2

They traveled by the light of a full moon, walking the horses slowly over the washes and endless convolutions of the badlands. The temperature turned bitterly cold, and by dawn, the horses were stepping so slowly that the men could have gotten down and walked faster.

Johnny slid down and began stripping off his saddle.

"We've still got an hour before it warms up," said Toomey. "They can go some yet."

"No sense to that," said Johnny.

He removed the bridle and slapped the horse's flank, and the horse stood there a moment, then walked off.

"You turning him loose?" asked Toomey.

"He's got a chance," said Johnny. "A horse has got a nose for water. Maybe he'll find some and make it to the mountain."

Toomey slid down and unsaddled his own horse, and it moved off after the other one, head down.

Johnny shouldered his saddle and gear.

"What now?" said Toomey.

"Yonder's a ledge of rimrock. There'll be shade there. We'll sleep it off and cross the open sand tonight. We'll be in the foothills by dawn tomorrow."

They staggered a mile to the rimrock, and by the time they got there, the sun was hot. Toomey threw himself down, and Johnny sat beside him and opened the canteen.

"One swallow," he said to Toomey.

Toomey drank carefully and handed the canteen back.

"You weren't serious when you said you'd pull out, were you?" asked Toomey.

"The nuggets pay for the trip. I'll get another horse in town and head back."

"What'll you do?"

"Winter's coming. I'll sign on with the Army as a scout. The Army is good for wintering in."

"Chase Apaches all winter? Eat dirt, sleep on the ground, get shot at? Is that better than a quarter share of a hundred thousand? You could buy the best ranch I've seen out here for the kind of money you'd get."

"At least with Apaches, you know they're going to try and kill you."

"I said I wouldn't cheat on you again, and I never had a stomach for killing."

"No. I've made my choice," said Johnny.

They walked west by night, carrying their saddles, and Toomey kept up. He was a tough little rooster. They ran out of water the second night and were so exhausted when dawn came that they fell where they stopped. Toomey looked west, and the mountain was still far off.

"We can't make it," he murmured.

"Another night's travel," said Johnny.

His tongue was swollen inside his mouth, and he could not work up saliva to soothe the dryness. They slept fitfully in the sun, and Toomey ran a temperature and moaned in his sleep, and that night they started out minus the saddles. It was obvious they could not carry anything and make it. Toomey staggered often and fell down, slowing them, but quitting never crossed his mind. Johnny found a century plant and cut its water-bearing core out with his bowie knife, and the moisture gave them strength. They chewed the fibrous flesh of the plant and sucked it dry to get every drop.

They began to realize they were climbing, and by the time dawn came, they could look back at the desert below them, and they knew they were on the mountain. Johnny kept Toomey on his feet, and they climbed painfully until they were in the trees; scrubby, stunted things, but there was shade. It was twenty degrees cooler there, and they slept half the day, and when they awakened, they were refreshed.

"No more desert for me," said Toomey. "I didn't think we'd make it."

"We came close," said Johnny.

There was no way to go but up, and they climbed, their feet swollen and sore inside their boots, and they came to a high ridge overlooking the town at dusk that day. Johnny stopped and looked down on the mining town two miles away, and Toomey stopped beside him, and they could hear a dull pounding in the air.

"Stamp mill," said Toomey.

Lamps were being lit in the town as dark came on, and it was a welcome sight.

"I'm going to hire a tub by the hour and soak in it," said Johnny. "Then I'm going to eat a side of beef and sleep for a week."

"Can't go straight in," warned Toomey.

"Why not?"

"Orders. We've got to look up a party first."

"Where?"

"He's beyond town. Over the next ridge there."

"Not me. This is where we say goodbye."

"You've made up your mind?"

"Yep."

"I don't see how I can force you," said Toomey.

"I don't either. Can you make it alone?"

"I'll make it. If you change your mind, you'll be seeing me in town."

"If I change my mind."

"You're making the biggest mistake of your life. Two days from now, you could be a rich man."

"Some ways of getting rich are too expensive," said Johnny.

Toomey saw that it was no use.

"I'll go around and pick up the trail on the other side," said Toomey.

"Good luck," said Johnny.

"If you see me, pretend you don't know me," warned Toomey. "Understand?"

"Yes."

Toomey turned and moved off, and Johnny started down into town alone.

3

Lucky was the name, and it was a plain, ugly town. Johnny staggered up the short main street on swollen feet, looking for a bathhouse and a place to flop, but he did not see either. None of the log buildings were finished. They had canvas roofs or sidings with the flaps drawn back, and Johnny could see men in every stage of bachelor domesticity, cooking, eating, sleeping, and quarreling. There were no women in sight. The street was ground to silt by the wheels of ore wagons, and Johnny's boots sank into the powder above the ankles. The constant pounding of the stamp mill crushing ore on the hill beyond town was loud in his ears, and Johnny wondered how the miners could stand it. He turned in at a place with planks laid across barrels that advertised itself as a saloon and walked unsteadily to the bar. A few old, stained poker tables lined one wall, and a coal-oil lamp hung from the ceiling. A half-dozen men sat around drinking out of tin cups. The bartender watched Johnny's approach from under bushy eyebrows.

"What can I do for you, friend?" asked the bartender.

His voice was not unfriendly.

"Is there a hotel in this town?" asked Johnny.

He came under the light, and the bartender could see the sunburned face and cracked lips, and he realized Johnny was not just another drunk.

"Hotel, hell! There isn't a decent bed within a hundred miles," said the bartender. "Just get in?"

Heads turned toward Johnny, and the men in the saloon grew quiet.

"Yes," said Johnny.

"Through the desert?"

"Yep. Lost my horse two days out. Had to hoof it."

"You look like you could use a drink," said the bartender.

He poured whiskey into a tin cup and pushed the cup toward Johnny, who put his foot up on a two-by-four spiked to the ground for a bar rail and steadied himself.

"Well," said Johnny, "it can't hurt now."

He lifted the cup and drank, and the alcohol almost doubled him over.

"Guess I need water worse," he apologized. "Any place I can get a meal and flop?"

"I can fix you up with food," said the bartender. "Venison is all we got, but there's no place to flop. They're sleeping three to a bed in shifts here. There's a gold strike on, man."

"I can pay," said Johnny.

He reached into his pocket and let the gold nuggets roll out across the plank.

"It don't make any difference," said the bartender. "There just isn't a bed to be had. I'll bring your grub."

He went out the flap behind the bar, and Johnny poured himself another drink. He pocketed his nuggets and took his cup to go sit down at one of the deserted poker tables. The miners watched him in silence, but Johnny was too tired to pay them any mind.

The bartender came back with a tin plate of hot venison stew and a spoon, and Johnny dug in.

The men in the saloon sat watching him eat, sipping their whiskey and not saying anything. Johnny suddenly became aware of a new silence in the room, and he looked up to find a man in the doorway carrying a shotgun. Two others stood back in the night, almost out of sight, covering the first man, and Johnny put down the spoon carefully and placed his hands flat on the table.

The man with the shotgun was a professional. A handgun hung from his right hip under a frock coat. He wore a black hat, black string tie, and his white linen shirt was starched. He stepped inside the saloon, and the two men behind stepped in and took places on either side of the doorway.

"Keep your hands flat," said the gunman.

"What's wrong?" asked Johnny.

"I ask the questions. Now, what's your name?"

"You'd better answer nice," said one of the others. "This is Mick Fender."

"John Terrell. Are you the law?" asked Johnny.

"That's right. What are you doing here, Terrell?"

"Minding my own business."

"Take his gun," Fender told one of his men.

Johnny pushed himself a foot away from the table and sat straight.

"I don't give up my gun," said Johnny quietly.

The man stopped and looked at Fender, who swung the barrel of the shotgun to cover Johnny.

"He's going to take your gun," said Fender.

"No," said Johnny.

"I can blow you right out the side of the tent," said Fender.

"You won't get any answers that way," said Johnny.

Fender hesitated.

"Now tell me what this is all about, and maybe I'll listen." Johnny continued, "I'm a reasonable man."

Mick Fender did not lower the shotgun. He nodded to his men, who separated, one to each side, and the miners fell out of their chairs, hitting the dirt floor.

"All right," said Fender to Johnny. "You've got a pocketful of gold that doesn't belong to you. You've got some questions to answer. I don't care if you live to answer the questions."

Johnny realized that Fender meant it. The bartender must have sent someone out back after the law, and Johnny was too tired to make a run for it.

"I found the gold," said Johnny.

"Where?"

"Out on the desert. There was a dead man by a water hole."

"That's better. Now the gun."

One of Fender's men walked carefully to Johnny, and Johnny let him take the handgun.

"You're getting smart," complimented Fender. "On your feet."

They marched him outside and around back of the saloon, and Johnny did not like that.

"Where's the jail?" he asked.

"We haven't got one," said Fender. "This will do."

Several miners had followed at a distance, and Fender whirled on them.

"Scatter," he said.

They ducked back, and Fender turned to Johnny.

"How'd you get here?" he asked.

"Walked."

"Clear from that water hole?"

"That's right."

"What brought you here?"

"Just passing through."

"To where?"

"Texas."

"What part?"

"San Antonio, to join a cattle drive."

Fender seemed satisfied with that, and he held out his hand for the gold. Johnny gave it to him, and Mick Fender hefted the nuggets he had taken from Johnny while he thought about it.

"I'll keep the gold," said Fender. "You be out of town by noon tomorrow."

"That's all I've got," said Johnny.

"It belongs to Brooks Hall," said Mick.

"Was he the dead man?"

"Not hardly. Brooks Hall owns the mine this gold came from."

"How can you tell that?" asked Johnny.

"Brooks Hall owns everything here."

"You can't prove the gold came from here. It could come from anyplace."

"You can't prove it didn't," said Mick.

He put the nuggets in a coat pocket, watching Johnny's face all the while.

"How can I get a horse and grub to leave with?" asked Johnny.

"That's your problem. Just be gone by noon."

Fender turned on his heel, and the deputies started to follow.

"How about my gun?" asked Johnny.

The deputy with Johnny's gun hesitated.

"Mick?" he asked.

"Give it to him," he told the deputy, and to Johnny he said, "Don't try and get a horse with it."

The deputy handed Johnny his gun and they left, and Johnny stood alone in the dark. He was not tired all of a sudden, and he felt the anger rising in his craw as he rammed the handgun into the holster. A hissing noise made him whirl about, and he saw the bartender from the saloon standing in the half-light at the back of his tent. The bartender motioned, and Johnny walked over to him.

"I'm sorry they jumped you," said the bartender. "My cook went after Fender. Every other man's a spy for Fender and Hall. You didn't finish your supper."

"That's all right. I can't pay for it now, anyway."

"Wait here."

The bartender slipped inside and came back in a few seconds with another plate of venison. Johnny sat down on a box and ate, although his appetite was gone. He needed the food, and he knew that, but the meat was tasteless in his mouth.

"Who's Brooks Hall?" asked Johnny.

"He owns the town. Got it sewed up."

The bartender sat on a box and lit a cigar.

"Heard them warn you to leave town," he said.

"Don't know how I can without a horse."

"They don't intend for you to leave."

"Why'd he tell me to get?"

"To put pressure on you. Hall needs men. He

needs miners, and he needs bullwackers to drive the ore wagons. There aren't enough men here. He has patrols on all the roads to keep men from leaving, and he sent a party out to blow the water holes on the desert east of here. I'd like to leave, but I don't dare."

"He can't keep you."

"I'm afraid he can. When I first came, it was a roaring camp. Every other man had gold. I ran four gaming tables around the clock and cleaned up, then Brooks Hall arrived. He's a big man. I don't know how to describe it, but he's just one of those men who get what they want. He's an organizer, maybe a genius at mining law and a few other things too, but he's even more than that. You can't buck him. Everybody liked him at first. You wanted to be where he was, but I misjudged how really hard he was. When he got what he wanted, he just wanted more. He'll do anything to keep it all to himself. He's had men killed. I know it and so does everybody else, and when he took my dealers for his mines, I kept my mouth shut. Now I run my saloon alone and look for a chance to get out."

"Why doesn't someone report him to the territorial governor?" asked Johnny.

"Very few men get out, and those who do don't care to go to the law. Hall has most men in debt. A few have gone to the governor only to wind up in the federal prison at Yuma, and it's getting even harder to leave with winter coming on. Hall knows he has to hold his miners through the winter because nobody would come back in the spring."

"Winter's close on," said Johnny. "I could smell it at night out on the desert."

"Once it snows up here, it keeps on snowing. They've had as much as forty foot of snow on the pass above us."

Johnny stood up.

"Thanks for the supper," he said.

"What are you going to do?"

"If I have to leave, I'd better get started."

"You can't get far without a horse or a mule," said the bartender.

Johnny did not answer.

"I've got a feeling you think you know where to get a horse," said the bartender. "Don't try to take one from the mine corral. It's a sure way of getting killed."

"I wasn't planning on it."

"My name is Stiles, Harry Stiles," said the bartender. "If I can help, let me know."

"Johnny Terrell," said Johnny as they shook hands. "Thanks again for supper."

"Wait," said Stiles.

Johnny waited.

"You're really leaving," said Stiles. "I can tell. You've got some way to get out of here?"

"If you don't ask, I won't have to lie to you."

"I've got an offer."

"I don't want to hear it."

"Why not," said Stiles. "You're broke and alone. I've got money, lots of it, and I need help."

"Why pick on me?"

"You look like a man who can take care of himself."

"You just saw the law pocket my gold and tell me to get out of town. Does that sound like a man that can take care of himself?"

"I've seen saddle bums ride in here before. Mick Fender never did less than pistol-whip them and beat them senseless. He didn't touch you, and I think I know why. He guessed it would be a mistake, and I'd agree. He gave you back your gun, and he's never done that before. If you'd been a different man, he'd have made you beg for it. I want someone to lead me out of here before the snow sets in."

"How about Hall's patrols?"

"We wouldn't go north or east. It can be done by going west over the mountains."

"There's nothing but wilderness," said Johnny.

"Then you do know this country?"

"Maybe."

Stiles moved closer. He peered around them in the dark to make sure they were not overheard, and his voice was low but urgent. "If you leave, take me with you," said Stiles. "I've got close to . . . I've got a lot of gold hid, dust and nuggets from the gaming tables. I'll give you a share."

"You're taking a lot for granted," said Johnny. "How do you know you can trust me?"

"I've got to. I'm afraid Hall will decide to close me down. He's got his own saloon up the street, and if he closes me down, I'll have to go into the mines. I'd never live to spend my money."

"You're running scared," said Johnny.

"You don't know Hall and Fender and his hired guns. A dozen men have been killed outright or just disappeared."

While Stiles talked, his hand had gripped Johnny's arm, and Johnny had to pry the bartender's hand loose.

"I'll think about it," said Johnny.

"You won't leave tonight?"

"I'm beat. I'd better get some sleep."

"Go down to the end of the street on the left, near the creek, and you'll find a lean-to. There's an old man there that rents floor space. Tell him I sent you. There aren't any empty beds in town, but at least you'll get a blanket and have a roof over your head."

"All right," said Johnny.

"Come back for breakfast, and I'll fill you in. There's lots you should know if you intend to stay alive in Lucky."

Johnny walked the length of the street, and he could see the difference in the town now. It was not like any other gold camp he had known. The men he encountered were quiet, almost sullen. There was not the hell-bent, roaring atmosphere in the air that most gold towns had after nightfall. He passed a saloon with a fiddle and piano going, and with the sounds of gambling and drinking, but the men inside appeared more desperate than festive. The sign over the open door read, "Golden Ram Saloon, Brooks Hall, Prop."

Johnny found the lean-to and got a dirty blanket from a half-blind old sourdough, but the room smelled of the unwashed bodies of a dozen men sleeping in rows on the floor, and Johnny took his blanket outside. He walked away from town and made a bed on the other side of the creek and fell asleep the moment his head touched down.

An hour later, Mick Fender and the two deputies entered the lean-to with a lantern. They moved from one sleeping body to another, their guns drawn, but they did not find the man they were looking for.

4

Johnny Terrell washed in the cold water of the muddy creek. The water was thick with mine tailings that stung his cracked lips. The sun was high, and he judged that he had three hours until noon, but he felt refreshed and ready. He checked his gun and put fresh loads in the chambers, cleaned the barrel and moving parts, and walked back into town.

The old man took the blanket without a word, and Johnny started up the street. No one was in sight. The miners had gone to work at dawn, and the men who worked nights were asleep. The banging of the stamp mill was loud on the air as Johnny made his way toward a large corral a hundred yards from the tents. The corral covered about three acres, and there were horses in one section and about a hundred mules in a separate section. Men were busy harnessing mules to high-bodied, large-wheeled ore wagons while two men stood guard with rifles. Nobody paid Johnny any mind when he walked up. He approached a guard and stood watching.

"Spanish mules," observed Johnny.

"Small but tough," said the guard.

"Expensive and worth it. They last."

"You new here?"

"Yep."

"What do you want?" asked the guard. He was not unfriendly.

"Looking for a horse."

"Lost one?"

"Want to buy one."

"Out of luck, stranger. I'm not the one to see, but you're wasting your time."

"Who do I see?"

"Brooks Hall. His office is up at the mine by the sampler mill, but take my advice: Don't go up there."

"Why?"

"You look like a cowboy, not a mucker. If you don't want a shovel stuck to your hands, stay away from the mine."

"I need a job to pay for a horse," said Johnny. "Who can I see about that?"

"Ever been a freighter?"

"With the Army."

"Maybe you could get on as a teamster. Reason you can't buy a horse is we have to freight all our stuff in from New Mexico or Denver. Horses and mules is more valuable than gold or just about."

"Anybody else got any horses?"

"Nope."

"Nobody?"

"Let me give you a tip," said the man, and he lowered his voice. "If you go looking for a horse here, you're looking for trouble. Hasn't

Fender talked to you yet? How long you been in town?"

"I saw Fender last night."

"And you're not beat up? That is a caution. Now you'd better leave. Nobody's supposed to come near the corrals. I've got orders."

"Thanks," said Johnny.

"Don't mention it."

Johnny walked into town and stopped the first person he saw, a Chinaman dressed in a padded coolie suit and wearing a pigtail that hung down from under a cap that had no bill.

"Is there a post office here?" asked Johnny.

"No speak," said the Chinaman, and he pulled away and almost ran up the street.

Johnny walked to Stiles's saloon, and Harry brought him a cup of black coffee.

"Fender went looking for you last night," said Stiles.

"Why?"

"I don't know."

"He didn't find me," said Johnny. "Is there a post office here?"

"No."

"I thought I'd send for money. Can't I even get a letter sent out?"

"Sure. Costs an ounce of dust a letter. Hall has the mail franchise, but I doubt you'd get an answer."

"No telegraph, I suppose."

"No. You're stuck. Have you given my proposition any thought?"

"Not so's you could notice."

"Why not?"

"I'll be lucky to get out of here with my own skin, let alone sneak you out with me."

They were interrupted by the sound of a horse outside in the street, and Stiles became attentive. He crossed to the flap, opened it, and looked out.

"Another new arrival," said Stiles. "And this one's got a horse. Now you'll see how Mick Fender operates."

Johnny came to stand by Stiles, and he recognized Toomey right away. Toomey was riding a horse that had seen its best days, a worn-out old bag of bones that looked like it had just made the trip from Georgia in one jump, and Toomey appeared no better off. He got down in front of the Golden Ram and went inside, and it wasn't three minutes before Mick Fender and a couple of men came down the street and entered the saloon. Johnny heard loud voices and swearing and the crash of glass, and then Toomey came hurtling out of the saloon to land in the street in a cloud of dust. He was on his feet as fast as a cat, but Fender's hoodlums were on him too quickly, and they beat him to the earth with their fists, and one of them gave Toomey a vicious kick in the back. Toomey arched like the blade of a knife under tension, then doubled up and lay still, and

Fender ordered one of the men to throw him on the horse. They led the horse away with Toomey hanging head down, his arms swinging loosely, and Johnny stepped out and walked after them.

"Wait!" warned Stiles.

But Johnny did not stop. He picked up Toomey's hat from the dirt. "Fender," he called.

Mick turned slowly, and the others halted behind him. "You forgot the old man's hat," said Johnny.

"He won't need it," said Fender.

"Don't miss any bets," said Johnny. "Maybe you could sell it and get a nickel for it."

"I gave you one chance to leave town," said Fender. "You should have took it."

"I'm still here." Johnny stood with the hat in his left hand and his right hanging relaxed, slightly in front, and he had his weight on the balls of his feet.

"There are three of us," said Fender.

"You'll need them," said Johnny.

"You wouldn't get ten feet out of town," said Fender.

Mick was doing a lot of talking, but he did not really seem to be concerned, and Johnny realized he was being suckered. He started to move sideways to get a look behind, but he was too late. Stiles shouted a warning that was interrupted by another voice.

"Hold it, cowboy," said someone behind Johnny.

Johnny felt his back crawl. He turned his head slowly and saw the bartender from the Golden Ram holding a double-barreled shotgun.

Fender walked quickly to Johnny and hit him in the face. The blow did not travel twelve inches, but Johnny reeled back. Fender hit again with his left, and Johnny rolled with it and hooked back with his right and caught Fender a staggering blow on the side of the neck. If Mick thought Johnny was going to stand there and take a beating, he knew better now, and both men got their guard up and circled silently.

Fender threw a right, and Johnny ducked under it, but Fender came in behind his rush, and they collided and fell in the dirt, clawing at each other's faces and trying for the groin with their knees.

Fender's men came running, and others, too. This was a killing fight, one they wanted to see, and their faces mirrored a prurient excitement. Everything was forgotten in concentration on the two big men rolling in the dust. Fender was the first to break free, but Johnny was quicker to his feet, and he caught Fender with an uppercut as he arose, and Mick went over backwards. Johnny threw himself on Fender and got on top of him. He straddled Fender and put his knees down on Fender's arms, then he spit on his fist and swung roundhouse. The fist landed on the side of Fender's head with the sound of a wooden club on a ripe melon, and Fender's eyes rolled up into his head. He moaned as Johnny wound up again.

"Stop it," said a deep voice. The voice carried over the excitement and cut the air like wind snuffing out a candle.

The bartender hurried to step forward, and he hit Johnny over the head with the barrel of the shotgun, and Johnny fell forward and lay still. Neither Mick nor Johnny moved for a moment. The crowd had turned to look at a tall, expensively dressed man who had gotten down from a blooded horse and now stood watching Fender, who was beginning to try to sit up in the street.

"What happened here?" the tall man asked.

Fender blinked his eyes and recognized him. "A private fight," said Fender.

"I pay you to fight for me. Isn't that right?"

"Yes, Mr. Hall," said Fender.

"Looks like I'm paying the wrong man. He would have killed you."

Fender did not say anything.

"Bring him to me at the mine," said Brooks Hall.

"Yes, sir," said Fender.

Brooks Hall turned to his horse and mounted. He got up on that horse with a dash and style that marked him as a born horseman, and he sat looking down on the assembled mob with neither disdain nor recognition. When he rode away, he rode with a straight back, proud, even arrogant, and some there noticed that his knee-high polished boots had not even been made dusty when he had stood in the street. He was like that. They had long ago decided that Brooks Hall could not get disheveled even when working underground beside his miners, something he often used to do.

Fender's men got Johnny on his feet. They took his gunbelt off and walked him uphill toward the mine along with Toomey, who still hung head down over the horse. At the mine, high on the side of the hill, they tied Toomey's horse beside Hall's blooded mare outside the mine office, a large log house, and Fender went inside, while his men dumped Toomey on the ground. Toomey groaned, and Johnny knelt over him.

"You all right?" asked Johnny.

Toomey half opened his eyes, and Johnny's lips made a shushing motion, and Toomey groaned elaborately to signify he understood.

"He needs a doctor," Johnny told the guards.

"Ain't none," said one.

"I'll be fine," said Toomey.

He sat up, but his hand flew to his side, and he grimaced and caught his breath.

The door opened, and Fender stuck his head out. "Inside," he said.

"Can you walk?" asked Johnny.

"I can try," said Toomey.

Johnny gave him a hand up.

"Either that whiskey I had was bad, or I got kicked in the bacon by a mule," said Toomey.

"You got kicked by an animal, anyway," said Johnny.

"Move," said a guard. It was the one who had kicked Toomey, and Johnny looked at him to know him.

They walked inside a long, low-ceilinged room to find Brooks Hall seated behind a big desk. The walls were covered with plat maps, engineering drawings, and charts of figures. Ore specimens lay on every conceivable resting place, and Hall's desk was a litter of papers, documents, and account books. It was a workingman's desk. Hall was in his shirtsleeves, a paneled linen shirt with lace down the front and at the cuffs, and it was brilliantly white and hand-laundered. Johnny could see the man's muscles move beneath the linen, and he recognized a strong, well-muscled man when he saw one. Brooks Hall looked at Toomey.

"You," said Hall. "Come here."

Toomey walked forward until he stood in front of the mine owner.

"What's your name?"

"Toomey."

"Toomey what?"

"Just Toomey."

"What's your family name?"

"My paw neglected to tell my maw. I got passed around among relatives until I could be on my own, and by then, everybody knew me by Toomey. After so many years, it didn't seem worth it to make up more names. I've got along just fine on Toomey."

"Where are you from?"

"Georgia."

"Gold country?"

"Yes, sir. Not like this, though. You get more gold out of the ground in a day than we get in a year back home." Toomey walked to a shelf where ore specimens were displayed. He hefted a specimen and turned to Hall.

"Quartz," said Toomey. "It's not local. Probably came from California."

He picked up another. He studied it intently.

"Now here's something," he said. "Gold-bearing calaverite and Sylvanite. If this is a specimen from your mine, you are lucky. There's silver ore in it, too. Are you extracting the silver along with the gold?"

"Trying to," said Hall. "It's hard."

"There's a new cyanide process," said Toomey.

"You sound like you know mills. Do you want to go to work for me?"

Toomey hesitated.

"I've been looking for my own strike," he said.

"Everybody thinks they're going to strike it rich," said Hall. "A hundred thousand, two hundred thousand men are tramping the hills looking for the mother lode. Most have never been in a mine. They think they can pick gold up off the surface and be rich in a day. There's a story circulating back East that you can slide down Pikes Peak on a sled with rasps on the bottom and peel off a fortune as you go."

"I know what it's all about," said Toomey.

"Do you? After you find gold-bearing ore, it costs a fortune to develop it. How much do you figure it costs to start mining?"

"Depends. Maybe ten, maybe fifty thousand dollars."

"Not even close. It'd cost that to haul ore to the nearest mills. I had half a million sunk in Lucky before we ran the first ton through the crusher. Where would you get that kind of money?"

"Sell shares."

"Do you think you'd get eastern banks to finance an unproved mine?"

"It's been done."

"By men with something to offer. My ore assayed out better than any in these mountains, and there's enough to last a hundred years. Do you want a job or not?"

"What if I say no?"

"You can leave."

"That man there," said Toomey, indicating Fender, "was going to take my horse."

"He'll pay you for it," said Hall.

"How can I get out of here on foot?"

"That's your problem. Winter's coming on. The first snow would overtake you before a week is out. Work for me, and you'll have a stake come spring."

"And in the spring, could I leave?"

"You have my word. I need men now. Especially skilled labor. I won't get any more men until winter's over, and a man who sticks by me will get top wages."

"Well," said Toomey, "I can't do prospecting with snow on the ground. I'll give it a try, but if I don't like it, I'll up and leave, even if I do have to walk."

"Fender," said Hall, "have one of your men show him where to bunk, then have him report to the mill."

Toomey left with Fender, and Brooks Hall looked at Johnny.

"What are you doing in Lucky?" asked Hall.

"Passing through. I told Fender, and he's probably told you."

"Yes, he has, and I think you're lying."

"That's your privilege."

"Nobody would come this way to get to San Antonio."

"I did."

"I haven't got time to argue. I could let Fender get the truth out of you. But I can use a top bullwhacker. Don't get surprised. I know you were a freighter for the Army. I hear everything that's said in Lucky. I'll give you a choice. Go to work for me, or I'll turn you over to Fender."

"That's not much of a choice."

"It's yours to make right now."

"I'll take it till I'm ready to go. Just like that old man, I'll walk if needs be."

"Nobody leaves Lucky till spring. You can count on it. When you go out, send Mr. Fender in."

Johnny left, and when Fender entered, he found Brooks Hall standing at the window.

"What do you think?" said Fender.

"Liars, both of them. I want you to check the old man's back trail. See where he came from."

"His horse was beat. Had red mud on it that could only have come from over on Brush Creek, which is the way he said he came."

"Check it out anyway. Did you search him?"

"Yes. That's when the trouble started. We had to calm him some."

"Was there anything on him?"

"No, and nothing on the horse."

"Anything new on high-grading?"

"No."

Brooks Hall turned to Fender deliberately.

"I'm going to give you 'til the end of the week to find the men who are high-grading and the place where they smelt the ore."

"I'm doing my best."

“If that isn’t good enough I’ll get a man who can. I didn’t develop the Lucky to let the muckers steal me blind. I want those high-graders, Mick. I’ll hang them up for the others to see, and if that doesn’t stop it, I’ll hang some more.”

“Miners are valuable.”

“Not as valuable as gold,” said Hall.

5

Johnny spent the day harnessing and unharnessing mules. The ramrod of the freighters would not trust him to drive yet, and Johnny fed mules, rubbed them down, helped the blacksmith, and generally did what he could see had to be done. The workday lasted from dawn to dark, and when he quit, he stood by the big corral and watched the miners come down the mountain. Each miner carried a lantern, and the swinging lights made a long ghostly trail as the men walked slowly and silently down the winding path to town. It was a beautiful sight, sad and beautiful.

Johnny washed in the creek and joined the teamsters for a common supper. They were fed out of huge pots by an indifferent cook, and the grub was terrible. After supper, he had a cigarette and strolled through the camp of tents and half-built log cabins, and he knew that it would be a hard winter. There was not enough wood close by to heat so many men, and the tents would not afford much protection, and there was already a tang in the air of winter's coming. Johnny kept an eye open for Toomey. He saw Toomey sitting before a tent with other miners, and Johnny stopped to drop his cigarette in the dust and grind it out under his boot. When he was sure Toomey had seen him, he walked on down to the creek and waited in the dark. In a few minutes, Toomey followed, and they moved off further from camp.

"Anybody see you come here?" asked Johnny.

"No. Do you think they suspect us?" asked Toomey.

"That Brooks Hall is no fool."

"Change your mind?" asked Toomey. "Going in with us?"

"Yep, but not completely. I'll go partway."

"What do you mean?"

"I'm not going to winter here. They're not hauling in wood. Too busy hauling ore. A lot of men are going to be consumptive come spring, and I don't want to be one of them. I'll help as far as getting out is concerned, but I don't like robbing the mine."

"Don't see how you can do one without the other. If you're going to chance breaking out, you might as well get paid for it."

"I'm not against getting rich," said Johnny, "but if I know one thing about that Brooks Hall, he's tough. You maybe could take his gold. Keeping it's another matter."

"Sorry, Johnny. If you go in with me, you go all the way. I wouldn't want you pulling out at the wrong time. How do I know you won't let me lead you to the man with the horses, only to see you help yourself and pull out? It's all or nothing."

"I don't know," said Johnny doubtfully.

"Depends on how bad you want to get out of here," said Toomey.

"Think you can pull it off?"

"We'll pull it off."

Toomey seemed confident.

"Who else is in on it?" asked Johnny.

"You'll meet them soon if you want in."

"When are you going to try it?"

"Right away."

"How soon?"

"We're waiting for Hall's mine superintendent, a man named Owen Kearns. He runs the smelter where the gold is stored. Kearns went to Santa Fe for supplies and labor. He's overdue now, but the day he comes back, we hit. There's over a hundred thousand in gold bars stored at the smelter, waiting to be shipped to Denver."

"What's your plan?"

"I'll let my partner tell you. It can't fail."

"When can I meet him?"

"You're in?"

"I'm in," said Johnny.

"I'll take you to him," said Toomey.

"Now?"

"There's no time to waste."

Toomey led, and Johnny followed along the creek bed around town. When they were clear of the tents, Toomey headed uphill, and Johnny noticed the old man was holding his side.

"Kidneys hurt?" asked Johnny.

"It's nothing," said Toomey.

But Johnny could tell the old man was in pain where Mick Fender's boys had kicked him.

They climbed steadily for an hour and stopped to rest. The town was in a valley completely surrounded by mountains, some of them above fourteen thousand feet, and they could look down far below to where the town of Lucky nestled in the bowl of the valley. They could barely see the lights twinkling there, and it looked like a pretty place from that distance.

"Who am I going to meet?" asked Johnny.

"You'll find out soon."

"Where'd you know him from?"

"Mutual friends," said Toomey.

Toomey started climbing again, and Johnny had to scramble to keep up. The old man was tough, all right. Toomey led them to a field of boulders, a vast area of rocks as big as houses, that had been left behind by a giant thaw after the ice age. The boulders were tipped every which way, leaving no pathway through them. They were piled one on top of another, some square, some jagged, and they covered an area of a square mile.

"You're not going through there in the dark?" questioned Johnny.

"Got to," said Toomey. "It's the only way to approach the cabin without leaving a trail. A man doesn't leave sign in solid granite."

They started in, picking their way around massive stones, climbing over others, scrambling to keep their balance. A fall down into the cracks between boulders would mean a broken arm or leg. Toomey chose a course due west, and when they came out on the other side, they were in tall timber out of sight of the valley.

"How far?" asked Johnny.

"Just a small piece now. We'll be back in Lucky in plenty of time to go to work."

"It'd be nicer to be back in time for some sleep."

In ten minutes, they came out of the trees into a mountain meadow. Johnny could make out a small cabin in the aspen trees across the way, but the cabin was dark. Toomey put his hands to his mouth and gave a fair imitation of a hoot owl. There was an answering hoot, and they started across the meadow. The door of the cabin opened, and a shaft of light spread over the ground. A man stood in the doorway waiting for them, and another man came around from the side of the cabin. He was carrying a rifle.

"Who's that with you?" asked the man in the doorway.

He had a hard voice, and his hair was cut so short his head looked shaved, emphasizing the bold lines of his face. He was going on sixty, but he looked fit.

"This is Johnny Terrell, Mr. Pejack," said Toomey. "He's a friend."

Pejack looked Johnny over for a long moment.

"Better come inside," he said.

They followed him inside, and the man with the rifle went back to his lookout somewhere behind the cabin.

There were three men inside: a Mexican, a cowboy, and Pejack, and Johnny did not like the looks of any of them. They were hardcases, and he felt naked without his gun.

"Toomey," said Pejack, "you'd better have a reason. A good reason."

"Johnny brought me to Lucky," said Toomey. "He knows something about our plans."

"Why didn't he come up here with you yesterday?"

"He wasn't sure he wanted in."

"But now he's sure?" asked Pejack.

Everybody stared at Johnny.

"What made you change your mind?" asked Pejack.

"I met Mick Fender," said Johnny.

"He's not notorious for winning friends," agreed Pejack.

Pejack turned to Toomey.

"You lied to me."

"I know it," said Toomey. "When Johnny backed out, I didn't dare tell you about him."

"What if he'd gone to Brooks Hall?" asked Pejack.

"Look at him and say he'd have done that," said Toomey.

"No, I guess not, but it don't make any difference," said Pejack. "I've gone to a lot of trouble. I've had to be careful, and I don't want any mistakes now that I'm so close. Mistakes can get a man killed."

The Mexican had not paid them any mind. He was lying on a bunk against the wall, and he did nothing more than glance up at the words.

The cowboy was sitting at a table playing sol, and he stopped playing to watch. Pejack was wearing a gun, and Johnny would not put it past him to kill.

"A second mistake won't correct the first mistake," said Toomey.

"What makes you think that would be a mistake?" asked Pejack.

"You must need him pretty bad to have him come all this way," said Toomey. "You can't get anybody close by to replace him now."

"You're right," said Pejack. "I need him. You use your head."

He walked to the table.

"This is Gantzel," said Pejack, introducing the cowboy. "He's good with guns. Over there is Bianco, who knows the land and the Indians. Toomey is a miner. Outside on watch is Goodhard, who is great with horses and mules. My full name is Orville Pejack, and I once owned this cabin. I owned all the land between the divide and the desert, including the valley where the town of Lucky stands. I had a small herd of cattle, and I raised a few crops, and then a fool cowboy found gold on my land. Do you begin to understand?"

"I think so," said Johnny.

"Come and sit down," said Pejack.

There were only two chairs, and Pejack looked at Gantzel, and the cowboy got up and went to sit on a bunk. He glanced once at Johnny with dislike and then began laying out a new game of sol.

"Gantzel is a sour man," said Pejack, as Johnny took a chair opposite him. "I don't know if he's killed so many men because he's got rot in his soul or if he's become rotten from so much bloodletting."

Johnny did not say anything.

"This was a line cabin once," said Pejack, looking about him. "My house was on the hill-side above Lucky. Brooks Hall and his mill super live there now. I had a wife. We weren't interested in gold, and I discouraged the first few prospectors, but word got out. That fool cowboy told stories in Denver, and I couldn't stop the stampede of miners. They dug everywhere. My cowhands joined the miners. My beef were shot and butchered. I tried to be everywhere at once to protect my range, and when I was gone, some drunken miners molested my wife. There was nothing to do but what I did. I killed a miner, and

I went to jail. No sane jury in the world would have convicted me, but my land was valuable to others. Wealthy men like Brooks Hall wanted the gold in the guts of my land, and they sent me to Yuma Territorial Prison for four years. I got out in two, but my wife had died, and my title to the land was no good. While I was in prison, Brooks Hall had sewed it up legal. He even owns this cabin. Lawyers told me to forget it. Go away. Start someplace new, but I'm sixty, and there's no reason to start over. My woman's gone, and there weren't any children."

"So you're going to get even," said Johnny.

"Revenge is part of it," admitted Pejack. "But if it were revenge alone, I'd fail, and I don't like to fail. As I said, I'm sixty years old, and it's too late for me, but with money, a new start is possible. I want to live out my years the way I could have if there hadn't been gold in Lucky. I'm going to take my share and live in Mexico. I'll have a ranch in a warm climate, take a young woman, have children, and I'll leave everything to them. Latins are a warm race, eh, Bianco?"

"The girls in Mexico will welcome you," said Bianco.

Bianco did not look up but took out a long, thin throwing knife and began cleaning his nails. He had good hands.

"Bianco was in prison with me," said Pejack. "So was Gantzel and Goodhard. We heard about

Toomey from friends. Toomey has not yet been in prison, but he should be. He can make lead into gold and gold into lead. He's a magician with gold. And you, Mr. Terrell, what can you do?"

Johnny shrugged.

"He's a magician with a handgun," put in Toomey.

"Has he had practical experience?" asked Pejack.

"I saw him perform in Kansas," said Toomey. "That's why I asked him to lead me here. We can use him."

Gantzel was looking on with interest now.

"We have a gun," said Pejack.

"He's been a freighter and scout with the Army," said Toomey.

"We have a bullwhacker, and we have a guide," said Pejack, and he turned to Johnny. "Is there anything you have to add?"

Johnny felt himself on trial. Pejack was desperate enough to have him killed if he was in the way.

"You might lose any one of five men," said Johnny. "I don't know how you plan to get the gold, but it won't be easy. If you lose any one of three, you're in trouble."

"True, but if there's shooting when we take the gold, the odds are that we won't make it anyway. We've got to take it by stealth, or we're lost. Anything else?"

"I'm only interested in getting out of Lucky before winter," said Johnny. "I don't care how, just so I don't end up dead. You could kill me, but that doesn't help you any. On the other hand, I may come in handy."

"You say you were a scout for the Army?" asked Pejack.

"Under General Miles."

"What do you think of him?"

"He's a good Army general but a terrible Indian fighter."

"Why?"

"He doesn't know Indians. He underrates them."

Pejack looked at Bianco, and the Mexican nodded in agreement.

"What work have they got you doing in Lucky?" asked Pejack.

"Harnessing mules."

"Do you work with the horses too?"

"Yes."

"We'll need horses. All right, Johnny, you're in. You'll get a small share but not what the rest of us get. Enough to make it worthwhile. I'll tell you something about it."

"Do you have to tell him?" asked Gantzel.

"We may move tomorrow," said Pejack. "He has to be ready."

"I don't like it. He may be a spy for Hall."

"You don't have to like it."

Pejack spoke softly, but it was settled, and Gantzel gave Johnny a look of hatred, but he shut up.

"We have to act fast because it's already snowed once on the divide and we're leaving by that way," said Pejack. "Once it snows bad, we can't get over, and there's no other way to go. To the north are towns and sheriffs. To the east is the desert. South of here, the land is just as bad, and we can't carry five hundred pounds of gold across badlands where it's so open. We've got to go west over the divide."

"That'll take some packing," said Johnny. "A mule can't carry more than two hundred pounds of that kind of weight."

"Goodhard is a packer," said Pejack. "Bianco will guide us and deal with the Indians. He can speak Ute, Comanche, and Apache—the three tribes we have to worry about."

"How do you get at the gold? It must be guarded, and there are a thousand men in Lucky. One shot and they'll come running, with Mick Fender and his boys in the lead."

"The mill superintendent is the only one allowed in the sampling room where the safe is. He can come and go as he pleases. The safe is big, too big to blast, and besides, the noise would attract attention. We're going to take the superintendent. He'll get the gold for us without a sound, and that's Gantzel's job. He can make a man do anything, and Owen Kearns is not a brave man."

"This Kearns is out of town?" asked Johnny.

"Yes, and he's due back. Should have been back two days ago. You and Toomey were late. I told Toomey to be here a week ago."

"We had a little delay," said Toomey.

"Will you wait outside?" Pejack said to Johnny.

Johnny got up and walked to the door.

"By the way," said Pejack, and Johnny stopped. "If you should try and contact Brooks Hall, you wouldn't make it. You'll be watched wherever you go in Lucky."

Johnny went out and closed the door, and Pejack turned to Toomey.

"I like him," said Pejack. "He's an honest man, but honest men don't always work out in a thing like this. Where did you meet him?"

"In a string town in Kansas. He was playing poker when I stopped off in a saloon on my way through. There was an argument about a man going light in the pot, and the accused man went for a gun. Johnny was quicker, much quicker. The dead man had friends, and I followed Johnny when he had to run for it."

"He ran?"

"Only when it got too hot. He had to fight his way out of the saloon, and he used his fists for that. I admired how he kept his head and didn't do any more killing than he had to. They cornered him in a rooming house across the street, and he held off fifteen or sixteen of them till I brought a horse to him in the alley. He didn't need no invitation to ride. He came out a side window like a stampede of miners for the gals on Saturday night, and we rode. Oh, how we rode!"

"You took a chance," said Pejack.

"It was worth it. He got me across that desert, and I'd have died without him to lead me."

"So you're even with him," said Gantzel.

"I guess I am," said Toomey.

"I still don't like it," said Gantzel. "He could turn us over to Brooks Hall as a favor. Hall would thank a man for telling about us."

"Johnny's not that kind," said Toomey.

"I don't think he is either," said Pejack. "He can be useful to us, but we'll watch him. Are you all set up, Toomey?"

"I'm ready," said Toomey.

"Stay away from our man in Lucky," said Pejack. "I don't want anyone to connect you two."

"Don't worry about me."

"It's late. You'd better get back before you're missed and don't come here again."

"I won't."

"We hide in the boulder field below by day," said Pejack. "There's nobody here in daylight. If you want to contact me, send word by Goodhard. One day, two at the most, and we'll be on our way."

Toomey went out, and he and Johnny started down the mountain.

"Only one thing puzzles me," said Johnny.

"What's that?"

"Your job in this. Pejack didn't explain what you're supposed to do."

"I can't tell you," said Toomey.

Johnny did not press him. He knew it was an important part of the puzzle, or Pejack wouldn't have sent for a man a thousand miles away.

6

The miners were rousted out before dawn and sent to breakfast by a loud whistle from the mill. They stood in line in the dark patiently, sleepy-eyed and quiet, and Johnny was sleepier than most. He caught sight of Toomey once from a distance and wondered how Toomey could be so chipper on so little sleep. Johnny ate a little of the slop called breakfast and reported for work.

The foreman was waiting for him.

"You Terrell?" asked the man.

"Yep."

"Get on down to the horse corral and pick out the best saddle broncs you can find. Fender's going out on a scout. He'll need a half-dozen horses."

Johnny started to turn away.

"And while you're there," said the foreman, "look over the stock and see what you think of them."

"What's your name?" asked Johnny.

"Goodhard," said the foreman.

He smiled and walked off, and Johnny watched him go, wondering how many of Pejack's gang worked for Hall. Johnny went to the corral and saddled six horses, and while he was there, he studied the stock. There were a couple of dozen good ones in a string of a hundred, and Johnny picked out the best. The gang must be planning to take out by horseback, he guessed, and he thought that it would be rough on horses, packing five hundred pounds in gold over the high pass.

Fender and his men came for the horses early, and Mick Fender hardly noticed Johnny. They rode in the direction of the boulder field and line shack above town, and Johnny watched them go and went to harnessing mules.

Goodhard stopped beside Johnny once in mid-morning.

"Fender rode up toward the line shack," said Johnny.

"I know," said Goodhard. "Don't worry about Pejack. He'll lead Fender a merry chase. He's been here all summer, and Fender's never got a whiff of him. Don't sell old Pejack short. He's smart, or we'd never have come here with him."

The morning dragged by, and then the afternoon went even slower, and toward dusk, Johnny heard a commotion from town, and he looked up from his work and saw Mick Fender and his men riding into camp from below town. They were leading a freight wagon, riding hard, waving their hats and shouting.

Men started running down the mountain, tossing their hats and "yippeeing" loudly.

"What's up?" Johnny asked a bullwhacker.

"Freight wagon from Santa Fe."

"What's so big about that?"

"Fresh whiskey and food, but I never saw everybody this riled up about the wagon before. Let's go see."

They joined the men hurrying into Lucky. A rider bolted uphill to the mine, and after a minute the mill whistle began to blow shrilly, and everybody that could walk was headed for the tent town.

"A woman!"

"Jesus, a woman!"

Men were shouting it and yelling and dancing in the street, and they wore silly grins on their faces for the sheer pleasure of it. A woman sat on the front seat of the freighter beside a handsome man, but all eyes were on the woman.

She was not an ordinary female. She was beautiful.

"Married!"

Johnny heard men saying it.

"Owen Kearns got married and brought his woman to Lucky!"

It was a time for rejoicing.

Someone shot off a gun into the air, and then another, and the crowd gave out a yell.

Owen Kearns stood up beside his bride and held out a hand for silence, but the crowd of men surged forward and their "yippees" cut off the sound of his voice.

"Shivaree!" shouted the miners.

Johnny was watching the woman's face. She had large, dark-brown eyes, black hair, and a full, red mouth. A traveling coat hid her figure, but Johnny knew without being told that it was lush and yielding, for this was no ordinary frontier woman. He concentrated on her face and watched as the woman smiled at the miners. She was used to them and their kind, used to their yells of appreciation. She was the best-known and most expensive whore in Santa Fe, and every man with the price had been with her, including many right there in Lucky, and Owen Kearns had married her.

"Shivaree!" screamed the miners.

They pulled Owen Kearns down bodily from the wagon, and his face went scarlet and then scared. The woman stayed calmly in her place, enjoying the excitement.

A rope was thrown over Kearns's shoulders, and he was led around behind the wagon and tied there, while another man jumped to the wagon seat and grabbed the reins.

The crowd parted, and the horses were whipped, and they took off up the street with the crowd running beside the wagon and Kearns staggering along behind at the end of his tether.

Saloonkeepers along the way handed out drinks, and a fiddler appeared from the Golden Ram and began to play and dance a jig at the same time.

Johnny followed on the edge of the crowd until he came to the end of the short street, where the wagon made a skidding turn and headed back. Johnny watched the wagon go by, and he caught the woman's eye. A frown crossed her beautiful face, and then it was gone, and she laughed out loud and turned, and half stood to look back at Owen Kearns stumbling to keep up in the boiling dust behind. And he was her husband.

"I'd give my right arm for some of that," said a leering miner.

"She's married now," said another. "Pull your tongue in."

"Yeah," said someone. "Keep your dirty mouth shut. She's the first married white woman in Lucky."

The crowd went rushing after the wagon, and Johnny stayed behind. It was getting dark, and as he passed Harry Stiles's saloon, Harry motioned for him to come in. Johnny entered and found they were alone.

"A drink to the bride?" said Harry.

"Why not," said Johnny.

He faced Harry across the plank bar. Harry poured two cups full.

"Here's to the rose of Santa Fe," said Harry. "Cleo Esteban Kearns. May she prosper."

They drank.

"Is that why she married him?" asked Johnny.

"Owen Kearns is a good mill man, but he can't

play poker, drink, or handle women. He's a baby among men."

"He's handsome."

"Yes, but weak. He's no match for Cleo. She'll eat him alive. That woman's a tiger, but Brooks Hall and she would make a match. They're both made of steel."

"Did you know her?" asked Johnny. "In Santa Fe?"

"Never had her kind of money."

"Thanks for the drink," said Johnny.

"Stop by any time. Your credit's good till payday."

Johnny walked outside to find the wagon pulled up in front of the Golden Ram. Kearns had been restored to his rightful place beside his bride, and he was drinking the health of the crowd from a tin cup. He was a little the worse for wear. Evidently, the fun had ended when he had fallen, because his suit was torn and very dusty, but he drank fastidiously. The crowd forced more whiskey on him, and he drank again, not so fastidiously this time, and Johnny could see what Harry meant.

Cleo refused a drink, and the boys did not press her. She had the effect of being superior without being insulting, and she was so beautiful that these rough men respected her every wish.

The fiddler was lifted up to the bed of the wagon, and the driver whipped the horses. The wagon headed for Brooks Hall's house up the mountain, and the men fell in behind. Some had found washtubs to beat on, and the din was ear-splitting.

Johnny did not follow. He saw Goodhard down the street, and Goodhard inclined his head slightly, then walked, and Johnny walked nonchalantly after Goodhard in the gathering dark.

7

Pejack could see the freight wagon enter Lucky from atop his hideout in the boulder field above the valley, and as soon as it grew dark, he and Bianco and Gantzel got their horses and descended to the edge of town. They dismounted in a grove of willows beside the creek and in a few minutes, Goodhard, Toomey, and Johnny waded the creek and joined them.

"What's it like in town?" asked Pejack.

"Dead quiet," said Goodhard. "Everybody's up to the Kearnses' house for the shivaree."

"Let's get started," said Gantzel.

"You're not going to try tonight?" asked Johnny.

"And why not, Mr. Terrell?" said Pejack.

"You won't be able to get close to Kearns tonight," said Johnny. "There'll be a thousand men around his place till dawn. You know what a shivaree's like out here."

"It's our best chance," argued Gantzel. "Everybody's drunk already."

Pejack looked at Goodhard.

"Goodhard?" said Pejack.

"The horses aren't guarded," said Goodhard.

"Toomey?" said Pejack.

"The mill guards are on duty. So is Hall.

He hasn't left his office to go to the party."

"What do you think, Bianco?" said Pejack.

"I'm with Johnny," said the Mexican. "It would be cruel to steal a man from his bride on his wedding night." Gantzel laughed, and Bianco looked at him.

"You are nervous," said Bianco. "You are tired of waiting, but sometimes patience is rewarded with success."

"Don't tell me, Mex," said Gantzel.

"Stop it," said Pejack. "I've heard you, and now I'll make the decision. It would be a good night to pull it off. The men will be dull and slow to act at dawn when they discover the gold is gone. On the other hand, Johnny is right. It will be hard to get Kearns alone tonight. He would be missed. The woman complicates things."

"Take her, too," said Gantzel.

"I was coming to that," said Pejack. "If we take him, she'll have to come along."

Johnny felt his stomach contract. The woman would receive Kearns's fate, whatever that was.

"We'll try tonight if the opportunity presents itself," said Pejack.

"Johnny, I've thought of a part for you, a way you can earn your share. We need time to complete our little plan after we have stolen the gold. We don't want them hot on our trail."

"You want a decoy?" asked Johnny.

"Yes, but we don't want you caught. You're to

harness a freight wagon at the corral. Goodhard will arrange that you're not seen doing it. Toomey has a load to put in the wagon. You're to drive the wagon toward the desert. Keep moving fast so that it is hours before they can overtake you, but abandon the wagon and head back here before you're caught. Understand?"

"Sounds easy as jumping off a cliff," said Johnny. "They'll trail me after they find the wagon."

"It's your job to see they don't follow your sign. You've had experience trailing. Can you lose them?"

"I can do it," said Johnny. "Where do I go when I get back?"

"We'll tell you, if we pull it off. Not till then."

He turned to Toomey.

"You've got a job to do. Get at it."

Toomey left, and Pejack pulled out a pocket watch.

"Seven o'clock," said Pejack. "If we don't take Kearns before midnight, we won't try it. The schedule's too tight to try much after midnight. You all know what you're to do, and if you're discovered, pull out and get the word to me."

They dispersed quietly in the dark, Johnny and Goodhard going toward the corral and the others heading off in different directions.

Goodhard made sure there was no one at the corrals, then Johnny quickly harnessed a team of the best horses. He wanted speed, not endurance, and he disregarded the Spanish mules. When he was done, he began to saddle a horse, but Goodhard came from where he had been standing guard.

"What are you doing?" said Goodhard.

"I'll need a horse to get clear with," said Johnny. "There'll be a mounted posse after this wagon."

"No horse," said Goodhard.

"It'll take me a day to walk back," said Johnny.

"We'll still be here."

"Why would you stick around after you get the gold?" asked Johnny.

"It's part of the plan."

"But they'll know they followed the wrong man."

"No, they won't," said Goodhard. "They'll think they got the gold back. It'll be days before they know it's not the real thing. Pejack figured this out to a fine edge. I've talked too much. Leave that horse go, and then hike up to Kearns's place and join the party. Mick Fender will notice who's all there. Keep your eyes open, and if I give you the sign, come back here and get the team and take it to the wagon that came in today. Hitch up and drive to the mill. You can be unloading the wagon while you wait for us. It'll be a good excuse for you to be up there at the mill."

8

Mick Fender knocked before he entered, and Brooks Hall's voice said, "Come in."

Fender walked into Hall's office and found the mine owner bending over the papers on his desk. A coal-oil lamp shed a warm light on the desk.

"You sent for me?" asked Mick.

"I want that shivaree stopped," said Hall.

"I'd get mobbed if I tried to stop it. That's the first we've had in Lucky since the Fourth of July."

"You've got enough men."

"My men are as drunk as the rest."

"Who's guarding the horses and the mill?"

"I've got the mill covered with two men. Goodhard's at the corrals."

"Double the guard. This is the kind of night for someone to try to steal horses."

"I'm lucky to have three sober men."

"Do it," said Hall. "You have the responsibility of the security of my mine and my property. If I lose one horse, you're in trouble."

"Have a heart," said Mick. "Let the men have their time. They'll wake up hungover and remorseful, and they'll be easier to handle for a few days. Keep them at work the way you're doing, and we'll have a riot before winter comes."

Brooks Hall sat back and put his pen down carefully on his ledger book.

"Listen," said Hall. "What do you hear?"

"The shivaree," said Mick.

"What else?"

"Nothing."

"That's right. What's missing? You don't understand, do you? The stamp mill is silent."

It was true that the stamp mill was silent for once, and even the roar of the shivaree could not make up for the loss of the sound of the giant crushers.

"I'm losing money," said Hall. "Every minute those stamps remain still, I lose money. If you can't stop that shivaree, I will."

He got up and put on his coat. He took a derringer out of the desk and put it in his pocket, and when he had put on his hat, he turned to Mick, who held the door open.

"How does she look?" asked Hall.

"Cleo? Beautiful. But then you know better than anybody."

"I should," said Hall.

"She's been waiting for you to show up."

"How can you tell?"

"She keeps watching the crowd. Only a hundred or so can get inside the house at a time. They've set up a keg in the living room, and she watches the faces of the men as they crowd through the door. I can't figure her marrying Owen."

"It's like her—unpredictable, devious—never what it appears on the surface with Cleo. She's got something else in mind."

"You and the Lucky?"

"Let's go find out."

Johnny stood outside the house in the crowd. Hundreds of men milled around drunk, and hundreds more crowded at the front door waiting to get in. As the men filed in, they received a cup of whiskey, drank to the bridegroom's health, and were crowded through the kitchen and out the back by the press of the mob behind them. Most ran around to the front again to take another turn.

Cleo sat in a chair against the wall and nodded to the men as they filed past. She had a smile for each and a word for those she knew, and she knew many by name. She had owned her own gambling hall in Santa Fe until the authorities had closed her down. She had hired only the prettiest girls, the sharpest dealers, and the best bartenders, and her place had been famous. The girls and the bartenders gave the men a fair shake, but the gamblers were questionable. Cleo had leased her tables to dealers who then gave her a percentage. If a dealer had a run of bad luck, she was only out a percentage and not thousands, but her dealers seldom lost, and after several bad gunfights and knifings, her place had been closed down.

Owen Kearns stood beside Cleo as she accepted the congratulations of the men, but no one paid him any mind. All eyes were on Cleo, and Owen resented it. After all, he was the bridegroom, and she was his. But he was powerless. The miners crowded in upon them, gaping at his wife, leering, licking their lips, and whispering to one another behind cupped hands. He hated it, and he drank. By the time Johnny got inside, Owen Kearns was sagging against the back of Cleo's chair, his eyes glassy, a sick smile on his too-handsome face.

Johnny took a cup of whiskey, but he did not drink, and he tried to get lost in the crowd, but Cleo looked directly at him.

"Johnny?" said Cleo.

Men turned toward Johnny as he faced her.

"Johnny Terrell," said Cleo.

She held her hand out toward him, and there was nothing to do but go to her.

"Hello, Cleo," said Johnny. And to Kearns, "Congratulations, Mr. Kearns."

Owen mumbled something that sounded ugly. Johnny ignored it.

"My best wishes, Cleo," said Johnny.

He was smiling, and she smiled back.

"Move on," said Owen.

"I hope you'll visit us," said Cleo, ignoring her

husband. "It's been a long time. You must have much to tell me."

"Not much," said Johnny.

"Quit bothering my wife," said Owen.

It began to grow quiet in the room, and Cleo turned to the fiddler.

"Play something," she said. "A wedding party should have music."

The fiddler stood up straight as best he could under the load of bad whiskey he carried and began to play.

Johnny moved away.

"Adios, Johnny," said Cleo.

"Adios," he replied.

"Do you have to be familiar with every saddle bum?" said Owen.

"He is an old friend," she said.

"Who isn't!"

She turned away, unperturbed, to watch two miners who were beginning to jig to the fiddler's music, and she clapped her hands in time to the tune. Others joined in clapping and dancing until the room vibrated with the sound of it, and then the crowd in the doorway fell back suddenly, and Brooks Hall entered, followed by Mick Fender and two gunmen.

The dancing stopped as if on cue, and the sound of the fiddle faded out, as the fiddler was the last to see Brooks Hall.

"Don't let me interrupt," said Hall.

He turned to Cleo in the silence and studied her, and she looked back at him evenly. She wore an emerald-green velvet gown cut low at the bosom, where a jeweled clip held the material just enough to expose the swell of her full breasts. The cloth set off her unblemished skin, and the diamond attracted the eye to the warm cleavage of her breasts, and Brooks let his eye linger there for a time that was too long to be polite.

"Perhaps Miss Cleo will dance for us," said Brooks. "She's famous for it."

The use of the "Miss" was intentional and insulting, and Brooks looked at Owen Kearns, but Kearns was too astonished to act, and Brooks went right on.

"Do one of the dances you did in Santa Fe," said Brooks.

It was an order.

Brooks looked at the fiddler, and the fiddler slowly raised his violin.

"Cleo," said Brooks.

Cleo rose calmly, even majestically, and turned to her husband.

"The first dance should be with the husband," she said. "If the fiddler will play a waltz?"

The fiddler hesitated, caught between them. Cleo did not intend to let the night descend to the level of a parlor-house revel, and she took her husband's arm, but Owen was too drunk to stand without the chair for support.

"He's out on his feet," said Mick Fender.

"The man said dance for us," said one of Fender's gunmen.

Cleo could not have survived in Santa Fe without wit, and she was not used to letting men treat her like a common whore. She turned to the miners.

"Is there no one who will dance the wedding dance with me?" she asked calmly.

There was silence until a man at the back spoke up.

"I will," said Johnny.

Johnny stepped out of the crowd and faced the fiddler.

"A waltz," he said.

The fiddler gathered his courage and struck up a waltz, and the miners fell back to make room as Johnny and Cleo circled in a very proper waltz that broke the ugliness of the mood. They danced so proudly that the moment was transformed, and it was again a real wedding party, and the faces of the miners inside the log house were glad.

Fender made a move, but Hall held him back.

"They'd kill you," said Hall.

The miners watched the woman circle the room. They crowded the windows and doors and watched in silence, and when the dance was done, they applauded.

"She's a lady," said one.

"She's a lady!" repeated another.

And it was agreed. She had won them completely.

Cleo went directly to Owen Kearns and leaned her head against him.

"I'm tired," she told them all. "Very tired. It has been a long day."

"A drink to the bride!" cried a miner.

"To the bride!"

"Make it the last one," said Brooks Hall.

He took a cup and held it up toward Cleo.

"To Mrs. Kearns," he said graciously.

The men drank.

"Party's over," said Hall.

And the men began opening a path toward the bedroom door.

Johnny helped Cleo guide the drunken bridegroom toward the bedroom among ribald jests and hoots. Once inside, Kearns collapsed over the brass bed, and those who could see laughed some more.

Johnny came out and shut the door, and men crowded around, beating on pans and yelling. Outside the bedroom window, another crowd made noise and shouted.

Johnny forced his way past Brooks Hall, and as he passed, Brooks called to him.

"Terrell, I want to see you in my office," said Hall.

"When?"

"Right now," said Brooks, and he turned to

Fender. "Get my stuff out of the bedroom. I'll sleep in the office."

Fender went to the bedroom door while Johnny followed Hall outside. Mick beat on the door until Cleo opened it a crack.

"Hall wants his stuff," said Mick.

Cleo closed the door without a word, and when she opened it again, she shoved Brooks's clothes into his arms. Mick could see past her into the room where Kearns still lay on the bed.

"Want me to come back?" said Mick. "I ain't the bridegroom, but I sure am the best man."

She looked him over coldly.

"A real man would know better than to ask," said Cleo.

And she closed the door in his face.

9

When they were alone in the office, Brooks Hall opened a small safe and got out a cut-glass decanter and held it up to the light.

"Twenty-six years old," said Hall. "Join me?"

"I've drunk it twenty-six minutes old," said Johnny. "I hate to ruin my taste for what I'm used to."

"You could be doing better. A man like you shouldn't settle for rotgut."

"I'm not ambitious."

"I think you are," said Hall.

He poured two drinks and handed one to Johnny, who took it.

They drank it neat, and Hall poured another.

"I like the way you stood up to me," said Hall.

"I'll bet."

"You're right. I don't like to lose, not at anything, but I can admire courage because it's valuable. It can be used."

"By people like you?"

"That's right."

They drank slowly, waiting each other out, gauging each other like two young gaming cocks looking for a weakness.

"You don't like me," said Hall. "Why?"

"Are you worried about it?"

"No."

"Then why ask?"

"I'm a winner," said Hall. "You are, too, I can tell. We're a lot alike."

"Except you're rich and I'm not."

"Everything evens out. The rich get ice in summer, the poor in winter. You could choose when you wanted your ice. Most men can't. You don't have to stay a saddle tramp."

"It's healthy outdoor work."

"Thirty dollars a month and keep? What are you going to do when your insides get too smashed up to ride? What's left? Become a cook for one of the big outfits? Not you. Not Johnny Terrell."

"What do you want?" asked Johnny.

"Right to the point. I like that in a man, too. I was going to offer you a job, but I see it's not much use."

"You're right."

"Have you ever been rich, Johnny?"

"No."

"If you've ever had money, big money, it's hard to settle for anything less. I don't mean payday money in Abilene after three months on the trail. I mean New-York, three-story-house, six-servants kind of money. Go-to-London-or-Paris kind of money. Eating off gold plate in restaurants where it costs a month's wages just for the wine. Buying clothes for women whose underwear is more expensive than feeding a laborer's family for six months. Ever smelled a woman like that? It's not woman-smell like you ever smelled before. More beautiful than a man could dream."

Hall stopped talking to see if he was getting to Johnny.

"You could have that kind of life," said Hall.

"How?"

"Take my offer."

"And do what?"

"Replace Fender. As you proved yourself, I'd move you up. This mine is only a start for me. I'll be turning it over to someone to run inside a year."

"How do you know I could do it?"

"Only a fool or a brave man who was perfectly convinced of his abilities would have done what you did tonight. The slightest hesitation or embarrassment on your part would have got you killed. You're not a fool, so that leaves the other."

"What if I won't work for you?"

"I'll have you killed."

"Still the same old choice," said Johnny.

"It has to be. I can't afford to have a man like you in camp working against me."

"Can I think it over?"

"Until tomorrow."

"That's not far off. What time is it?"

Hall looked at his pocket watch.

"Twelve-thirty."

"Give me twenty-four hours," said Johnny.

"Why?"

"It means a lot to me."

"You don't need twenty-four hours. You don't need twelve. You must have a reason."

"What happens if I say yes?" asked Johnny.

"Your first job would be to convince me that I can trust you."

"You mean take care of Mick Fender?"

"I knew you were bright."

"Has he got something on you?"

"Right again, but I wouldn't need to have him killed if he didn't, would I?"

"Someday you'd be hiring a gun to kill me," said Johnny.

He grinned at Hall, who smiled back.

"Not if you did your job," said Hall. "Fender's lost control. The men don't respect him anymore. Someday they'll mob him. I'm making a thousand dollars an hour in the Lucky, Johnny. I'll give you a percentage. I'm opening two more veins before spring. You'll be rich inside of a year. I'll give you your twenty-four hours, but if you try to double-cross me, I'll get you if I have to go to hell, and I'm not afraid of hell."

Johnny knew that the man meant it. Brooks Hall was without conscience.

"I won't disappoint you," said Johnny. "One way or the other."

• • •

Goodhard was waiting for Johnny down on the hillside. He stepped out of the shadows and fell in step.

"You better not be seen with me," said Johnny.

"What's he want?"

"I can't tell you now. Are they going to try tonight?"

"It's too late."

"When then?"

"Maybe tomorrow night. It's got to be done at night."

"Tell Pejack I can't wait past tomorrow night," said Johnny.

10

Johnny turned out for work at dawn with a lot of sick men, but where they had headaches and nausea, Johnny was only bone tired. He had not recovered from the trip across the desert, and in two nights, he had not had five hours' sleep. He could not keep going on that way much longer, and he longed for a chance to nap as the sun grew higher in the sky, but ore wagon after wagon had to be harnessed, and he worked like a dog all morning.

Cleo Kearns awoke beside her husband, realizing that the day was well started. She got out of bed without waking Owen, dressed, and went into the living room to find it cleaned and tidy after the night's party. A pig-tailed Chinese man padded into the room and bowed his head.

"Missy want breakfast?" he asked.

"Yes, please," said Cleo. "Did you clean the house?"

"Yes, I Mr. Hall boy."

"What's your name?"

"Sing Lee."

"Just coffee, please, Sing Lee."

He padded out, and Cleo went to the window to look out at the town below. The shivaree had lasted until dawn. It was a custom of the territory, a disgusting custom for young newlyweds to have to endure, but it had not mattered in her case. Owen had not revived to consummate their marriage.

Sing Lee brought her coffee, and she sat at a table listening to the stamp mill beat regularly. It was very loud this close to the mill. She was still at the table when the door opened, and Brooks Hall stepped inside.

"The blushing bride," he greeted her. "Is Sing Lee taking good care of you?"

"He had the house in order before I got up," said Cleo. "Have you had breakfast?"

"At dawn. We rise early here. How's Owen?"

"Still sleeping."

Brooks called for Sing Lee and had him bring another cup of coffee, and he sat down beside Cleo.

"Mind if I join you?" he asked.

"It looks like you already have," she said. "But that's like you. Brusque, never apologizing, a hard man. You can be charming too, as I should know."

"At which times do you like me best?"

"No flirting. I'm a married woman."

"How married?"

"For better or for worse."

"Really, Cleo?"

He was smiling, but she was not upset.

"You just can't believe any woman would

choose anyone else than you," she said. "You have a monumental conceit."

"I never asked you," he said.

"I didn't expect you to, and I wouldn't have waited for you to ask me. I married Owen. Let it go at that."

"You were a queen last night," he told her. "A queen of what, I don't know, but you were truly regal. You sat there like a monarch tending court. The men loved it."

"I like the men, I really do, and they know it."

"You can't stay here," he said.

"In your house? We'll find another place."

"I mean in Lucky. I'm shipping you out with the first freight."

"Why?"

"You'll cause trouble."

"With the men? I don't think so. They respect a married woman. Even one like me."

"I can't let you stay," he insisted.

"Is it you who are afraid?" she asked. "I know you don't respect marriage. Are you worried for yourself? You needn't be."

"What are you really here for?"

"To be with my husband."

"I don't think so," said Brooks and he stood up. "Owen isn't your kind. I think you have other ideas in that pretty head of yours."

"Owen is a sweet man. He's kind and handsome and good. You don't respect him because you think he's weak, and perhaps he is, but he only needs confidence. I'll make him a good wife."

"Somewhere else. Not here."

"You wouldn't send him away."

"I'd have to if he wouldn't agree to pack you back to Santa Fe."

"That's cruel."

"Practical. I want Owen in my office in fifteen minutes, drunk or sober."

He walked toward the door and stopped.

"Did you know that cowboy you danced with before last night?" he asked.

"Yes," she said.

"How well?"

"That's none of your business."

"I see," said Brooks.

"I thought you weren't jealous," she teased.

And by doing so, she told him more than she should have.

Owen Kearns went to Hall's office on weak legs. His head ached, and he could not hold anything in his stomach. Hall did not feel sorry for him, and he made Owen stand throughout the interview.

"Good morning," said Owen.

"Morning? It's almost noon. I suppose you'd like to have my congratulations, but you won't get them. You're a fool, Owen."

"Why?"

"Bringing that woman to Lucky was the worst

thing you could do," Hall said. "You didn't have to marry her."

"Don't insult Cleo."

"Come off it. You know what she is."

"She's changed."

"Don't be an ass. Women like Cleo don't change."

"I'm warning you, Brooks."

"What would you do? Kill me? You haven't the guts. Leave? Where would you go? You haven't got a cent, and Cleo needs money."

"I've got half a year's wages coming."

"How long would it last? You'd drink it up in a month, and Cleo would leave you."

Owen did not want to listen to Hall. He was afraid that it was true.

"Leave if you want. Take Cleo to Denver. She'd be back in a fancy house soon enough," said Brooks.

"Stop it," said Owen. "Don't say things like that. You don't want me to quit. You need me here. Who would run the mill?"

"I've got a new man from Georgia. The foreman tells me he knows more about refining gold than you do. Nobody is indispensable to me, Owen."

"I didn't mean for it to be like this. I didn't want to get drunk last night. Cleo has been good to me. She kept me sober in Santa Fe. She's not like you think."

"If you want to stay, you've got to send her away."

"Where to?"

"Back to Santa Fe, anywhere, I don't care."

"For the winter? It'll be six months before we get out in the spring!"

"Don't you trust her?"

"Of course."

"If she's all you say she is she'll wait for you."

"I can't do it."

"That's too bad."

"But why?"

"She's a bad influence. Look at the time we lost yesterday. I can't afford to have one woman in Lucky over a long winter. There'd be trouble, and we've got trouble enough."

"I'll keep her home. She won't go down into Lucky."

"Cleo wouldn't stay cooped up for a week, let alone a whole winter."

"I love her, Brooks. I can't give her up."

"All right, you can leave today. I hope you can get another job, but of course, I can't recommend you."

"You wouldn't tell?" said Owen.

"I can't recommend an embezzler or fugitive from justice."

"You're blackmailing me."

"I'm saving you from yourself. If you leave with Cleo, she'll drag you down. I'd rather see you return East to face that old embezzling charge."

"I'd almost rather take my chances than stay here."

"Almost?"

"You know I can't leave. When do I have to send her away?"

"I've just been waiting for you to get back before I shipped the gold to Denver. She can go with the gold train."

"When?"

"Tomorrow. That'll give you time to say goodbye. Take the day off. You look sick, and I need work out of you. The mill has run ten percent behind capacity since you left."

"It's good to know I'm useful," said Owen wryly.

"Of course you are, or I wouldn't make it so hard on you," said Brooks. "Let me show you something. Here are the financial reports."

He spread papers out on his desk, and Owen came close to look at them.

"When I discovered the big vein in the Lucky, I had to give away forty-nine percent to get backing from eastern banks. Forty-nine percent of millions. True, I retain control, and I'll still make a lot of money, but I'm dealing with hard men. I've got to satisfy pledges amounting to over a hundred thousand a month, and if I fall behind, I'll lose control. They'll squeeze me out completely. I had to borrow more last month when the mill broke down, and if I don't make delivery to the bank in Denver by the first of the month, I'll default on that loan and have to pay a penalty of thousands of dollars."

Brooks spread out other papers.

"Here are the production figures," he said. "You can see by the curve that I can't continue to produce enough to satisfy my creditors. We've got to open the Lucky number two and number three this winter. The mill and smelter have got to go on double shift. I need wood-cutting crews to bring in fuel for the winter. I haven't got enough wagons to haul ore to the mills and wood for fuel. I need every man I've got, and you go off and get married. Did you find out about labor in Santa Fe?"

"The alcalde said he'd send a hundred Mexicans but not at your price," said Owen. "They want to bring their women too."

"Next year," said Brooks. "We can't feed them all this winter. Someday there'll be a town here with all the amenities of civilization."

"If the vein holds out."

"It will," said Brooks.

He was silent for a moment.

"Maybe I could get Chinese coolies," he said, half to himself. "The railroad has a lot of coolie labor whose indebtedness hasn't been worked off."

"The men won't work with Chinamen."

"To hell with the men. Coolies work like dogs, and you don't have to give them much. I'll look into it. Go back to the house. Have your honeymoon, but I want you on the job tomorrow morning, early. I'll stay here tonight. Have Sing Lee bring my meals here."

"All right."

"And Owen, don't feel badly toward me. If we make it through the winter, I'll be in the clear, and I'll make it worth your while. We'll both be rich men, and you can go wherever you like."

"You've been promising me that for a year."

"I keep my promises," said Brooks. "I don't make idle threats either. You remember that."

When Owen returned to the house, Cleo met him at the door.

"What did he say?" she asked.

"You were right. He's sending you away."

"When?"

"Tomorrow. We're shipping the gold bullion to Denver, and you can ride with it."

"I see."

"I tried to make him let you stay."

"Come and sit down," she said.

She led him to a horsehair sofa, and they sat close together.

"He threatened to tell about that business back East," said Owen. "There was nothing I could do."

“I’m glad you told me about that,” said Cleo. “I don’t want you to keep anything from me.”

“I can’t let you go.”

He put his arms around her, and she pressed herself to him.

“We’ll think of something,” she whispered.

“Cleo,” said Owen.

His voice was urgent.

“Yes.”

They got up, and he led her into the bedroom and closed the door.

11

When Goodhard was told to have two wagons ready on the following morning, he knew that the time had come. It could mean only one thing: The bullion was being shipped out. He waited until the messenger left and then walked off by himself away from the corral. He went to an exact spot that was shielded from the town by boulders and took a mirror from his pocket. He manipulated the mirror until it reflected the sun's rays up toward the boulder field above town, signaling Pejack, and then he hurried back to the corral, hoping that they had seen his signal.

He found Johnny harnessing mules.

"Do you think you can get in touch with Toomey?" asked Goodhard.

"Not till supper."

"Bring him to the willows across the creek right after dark."

"Are we going to do it?"

"We've got to do it."

Johnny was ordered to take a load of wood up to the house by the mill. He hitched up a small wagon, loaded a cord of split stove wood into the wagon bed, and drove to the house. He was almost through stacking it when Cleo came out the back door.

"You were going to leave without seeing me," she accused.

"I didn't come calling," he said.

He started to get back up on the wagon, but she came close, and he hesitated.

"What are you doing in a place like this?" she asked. "You're no miner."

"Just stopped off. Liked it so well I stayed."

"Still the same old Johnny. I never could get a direct answer out of you. What happened to that ranch you were going to have?"

"I got the land."

"Where?"

"Montana."

"Cold country."

"Yep."

"Johnny, why didn't you come back?"

Johnny looked at her and saw that she meant it.

"I figured to," he said. "It took so long to get land, and then I set out to get money to stock the range. I'm still trying."

"You stopped writing," she said.

He shrugged.

"I would have waited," she said. "When you quit writing, I didn't know what to think. You could have been dead or found someone else."

"It took so long, I didn't think you'd be interested. Four years just to get the land. I wrote, Cleo, but then I didn't hear from you either."

She nodded.

"Mail gets lost easy," she said.

"No use crying over it now."

"I'm not crying," she said.

And she wheeled and ran back into the house.

Johnny stood for a moment looking down over the town and thinking back to when he had been a kid on his first trail drive over the hot, sunbaked lands of New Mexico and of the young, untouched Mexican girl he had met. He got up and drove the team slowly back to the corrals and went to work with a vengeance. He did not want to remember.

Johnny, Toomey, and Goodhard waited in the black of night for Pejack and the others.

"Maybe he didn't get your signal," said Toomey.

"If he doesn't come soon, I'll climb up and get him," said Goodhard. "But they've always got somebody on guard."

Crickets sang in the night, and the creek rippled smoothly, making just enough noise to cover their talk. A quarter moon shed pale light on the mountainside opposite them, and occasionally they could hear men moving about in town just across the creek.

Pejack came sliding down the bank into the willows without warning.

"Where are the others?" asked Goodhard.

"They'll be along with the horses," said Pejack.

"It's too early to chance bringing the horses down. What's up?"

"They're moving the gold at dawn," said Goodhard.

"Dawn hurts. It cuts our time down," said Pejack.

"Once they get that gold loaded, we're out of luck," said Goodhard. "They'll have a twenty-man escort."

"All right. How do we stand?" asked Pejack.

"Kearns is alone with the woman," said Goodhard. "Hall moved into his office. The Chinaman leaves about nine after he's cleaned up, so we can get Kearns any time after nine."

"Midnight then," said Pejack.

"What about the woman?" said Johnny.

"What about her?" asked Goodhard.

"If you take Kearns, what about her?" said Johnny.

"She'll have to come too," said Goodhard.

"What had you planned for Kearns after you were through with him?" asked Johnny.

They were silent for a moment.

"We can't take him along when we leave," said Pejack. "We'll be moving fast."

"And Cleo?" asked Johnny.

They did not answer.

"Count me out," said Johnny.

"You can't get out," said Pejack flatly.

"You're not going to kill a woman," said Johnny.

"We didn't plan on her," said Goodhard.

"Then you'll have to think of something," said Johnny. "You could turn them loose after we got free."

"To tell which way we went?" asked Pejack. "There are telegraph wires strung clear to Mexico. They'd be waiting for us when we came out of the mountains on the other side."

"Is it because you had a dance with her last night?" said Goodhard. "You can have her. One time."

"Shut up," said Pejack. "I don't like it either, but there's no other way."

"I haven't put in my two bits," said Toomey.

"Let's hear it," said Pejack.

"I'm with Johnny," said Toomey. "I won't go along with killing. We don't have to kill anybody."

"They'll hang us for stealing if we're caught," said Goodhard. "Killing isn't going to make it worse."

"We can hold them as hostages," said Toomey. "Once the alarm goes out tomorrow, the whole camp will be aroused. The miners would tear us apart if we harmed that girl."

"We're not counting on getting caught," said Goodhard.

"Let him talk," said Pejack.

"If we do have trouble, the girl is insurance. A hundred things could go wrong. I'd just as soon have a lever to bargain with. We can let her go when we're safe. We could keep her with us clear to Mexico."

"I'm beginning to like it," said Goodhard.

"Will you shut up?" said Pejack.

He thought about it.

"Johnny and I are together," pointed out Toomey. "We won't go along any other way."

"Don't threaten," said Pejack. "I'd be willing if it didn't mean more trouble. One girl among five men is bound to cause bad blood, and I understand she's a looker."

"Nobody's going to lay a hand on her," said Johnny. "And her husband goes, too. If we take Cleo, we might as well take him. He'll be careful to protect her."

"Maybe you're right. He has got more reason to help us if we've got her," said Pejack. "That's it. Unless something happens, we'll begin promptly at midnight. Anything else?"

"Yeah, Johnny here had a talk with Brooks Hall last night," said Goodhard. "I'd like to know what they talked about."

"Johnny?" asked Pejack.

"He offered me a job," said Johnny.

"What kind?"

"Fender's job."

"That's very interesting. What did you say?"

"I asked for time to think it over."

"Why?"

"There were conditions."

"What conditions?"

"I'd have to kill Fender," said Johnny.

"Do you think you could do it?"

"I'm not going to try," said Johnny.

"He could do it," said Toomey.

"This has possibilities," said Pejack. "I'd like to see Fender out of the way. He's a hard man to have on your back trail."

"Then you kill him," said Johnny. "Let's get this straight. I'm not going to kill anyone for Brooks Hall or you or anybody else."

"You've killed before," pointed out Pejack.

"That was different," said Johnny.

"There may have to be killing in this."

"I say there hadn't better be."

The two men stood staring at each other in the night, and Pejack was the first to look away.

"All right, let's get on with it," said Pejack.

Johnny and Toomey started back to town across the river, and Pejack held Goodhard back for a second.

"Keep an eye on him," said Pejack.

"Don't you trust him?" asked Goodhard.

"Do you?"

"I don't trust anybody where gold is at stake," said Goodhard.

The camp settled down for the night. Men ate, washed, and retired early to be ready for the next day's work. Some wrote letters, others dreamed.

Men with money in their pockets patronized the Golden Ram to have a drink and conversation. The piano player and fiddler took the stand and made music, and men with visions of improving their stake sat down at the faro and poker tables.

The street was quiet, and coal-oil lamps flickered inside tents, casting lonely shadows on thin walls. Johnny and Toomey parted at the foot of the street.

"Better turn in," said Johnny. "We've got a couple of hours till midnight."

"I'm so tired that if I went to sleep now, I wouldn't wake up for a week," said Toomey. "I haven't had four hours' sleep since we got here."

"I'll wake you."

"No, you might not get up yourself. I'll see you at midnight."

"Toomey," said Johnny thoughtfully, "do you think Pejack can pull this thing off?"

"Yes."

"You seem sure enough."

"Don't worry, it'll work, but I know what's on your mind. It's afterwards that I'm thinking about. Have you ever seen a man get hold of a fortune, sudden like?"

"No."

"It does something to him. Especially when it's gold. Gold brings out the real man, good or bad. Gold can be a disease. That's what makes miners. Once you get the gold fever, you're lost. You never get over it. I've known men to lose their wives and families and ruin their lives chasing gold, but that's nothing compared to what happens when they strike it. After we've got the loot is when I'll begin to worry. That's when I want you along."

"How do you know I'll be any different?"

"I know. That's why I picked you."

Goodhard and Johnny walked toward the corral. The quarter moon was hidden by clouds, and it was pitch black.

"Let me handle it," said Goodhard.

They could not see the guard, but they knew he was there.

"Hastings," called out Goodhard.

"Who's that?" came a voice.

"Goodhard," replied the straw boss.

The guard came out of the shadows between freight wagons and stood ready as Goodhard and Johnny approached.

"Everything quiet?" asked Goodhard.

"Sure," said Hastings. "It ain't two a.m. yet. What are you doing here? I don't go off watch till two."

"You and Johnny harness up a team," said Goodhard. "I want a wagon ready at the mill. We'll start loading before dawn."

The man hesitated.

"Go ahead," said Goodhard. "I'll stand guard."

Hastings leaned his rifle against a wagon.

"Yes, sir," he said.

Johnny brought the horses out from the corral one at a time, and Hastings began harnessing them.

"We want a six-horse team," Johnny told him.

"What's up?" asked Hastings.

"They're shipping the gold out tomorrow," said Johnny.

"That's a detail I'd like to have."

"Why?"

"For the trip to Denver. Ever been to Denver?"

Johnny worked on the bridles while Hastings did the harness, back band, hame straps, collars, and pads.

"Once," said Johnny. "I've been there once."

"I'd give anything to get out of here for a week."

"Just a week?"

"Oh, it ain't so bad. A man can save his money. By spring, I'll have enough put by to go back home and pay off the farm."

"Then you'd better stay out of Denver."

They got the team harnessed and led the horses to the wagon and hitched up.

"How come you're using horses? They usually use mules," said Hastings.

Johnny looked past Hastings to see Goodhard advancing toward Hastings' back. Goodhard held the rifle by the barrel, and he raised the rifle to club with it.

"Bend over here, and I'll tell you," said Johnny.

Hastings leaned forward, and as he did so, Johnny hit him crisply on the point of the jaw. The blow, coupled with Hastings' forward motion, was decisive, and Hastings fell forward into Johnny's arms. Johnny laid him on the ground.

"Why'd you do that?" said Goodhard.

"You could have crushed his skull," said Johnny.

Johnny bent down and stripped off the man's belt. He tied Hastings' feet together with the belt and used harness straps to tie his hands behind his back. He made a gag out of the man's bandana, and when he was done, Hastings could not move or make a sound.

"Who's supposed to relieve him?" asked Johnny, standing up.

"Nobody," said Goodhard. "They won't find him till dawn."

Goodhard pulled out his pocket watch.

"Plenty of time," he said. "It's just eleven-thirty."

They waited until ten minutes to midnight, and then Goodhard motioned to the high seat of the wagon.

"Climb aboard," said Goodhard.

Johnny got up over the big front wheel and took the reins.

"Drive to the side entrance of the mill. You know where the loading platform is?"

"Yes."

"Wait there and be ready to move. If anybody questions you, tell them you're just delivering the wagon for tomorrow."

"Where'll you be?"

"Close by."

Johnny clucked softly and shook the reins. The horses picked up their ears, and the lead horse started out. When Johnny was gone from sight, Goodhard picked up the rifle and walked toward Hastings. There was the sound of a blow and a grunt of air in the dark, and Goodhard came back out of the shadows and followed Johnny up the hill.

12

Cleo stirred in bed. The room was dark, and the sound of her husband's breathing was even and his body warm, and she turned to nestle close to him, then she froze. There was another sound in the room, and she came fully awake. Cleo reached out and put a hand on Owen's shoulder. He breathed shortly but did not awaken, and she shook his shoulder.

Owen Kearns sighed, but he was in a deep sleep and would not wake up. Cleo recalled that Owen had put a gun in the dresser drawer, and she sat up and laid back the quilt. The quilt made a rustling noise that sounded very loud, and Cleo waited a moment, but she did not hear anything else. She swung her feet over the side of the bed and started to rise, but she came in contact with something before she could gain her feet.

There was someone standing right next to the bed.

Cleo opened her mouth to scream.

Arms went about her, and a hand covered her mouth, and only a strangled cry came out.

"I've got the woman," said Gantzel.

A match was lit, and the men in the room could see Cleo struggling against Gantzel. Cleo's eyes were wide in hysteria as they looked up into Gantzel's grinning face.

Bianco crossed quickly to Owen and put a gun in his face, and as Owen started to wake up, the match went out. Pejack lit another, and Owen sat up looking into the muzzle of a Colt revolver.

Bianco pulled back the hammer with his thumb.

"*Silencio*," whispered Bianco.

Owen turned white. His eyes bugged out, and he looked like he would faint.

"Tell the woman to be quiet," warned Pejack.

Owen opened his mouth, but no words came out, and Cleo saw his fear, and she grew limp in Gantzel's embrace.

Pejack blew out the match.

"Light a lamp," said Gantzel.

"No light," said Pejack. "We don't want anybody coming up here."

Gantzel could feel the heat of Cleo's body through the soft material of her nightgown, and he wanted to look at her, but he would have to wait.

"Kearns," said Pejack.

"What do you want?" said Owen.

His voice was hoarse with fright.

"Do as we say, and you won't get hurt," said Pejack. "One mistake and we'll finish you."

"The woman, too," said Gantzel.

"Shut up," Pejack told him, then turned to Kearns again in the dark. "He means it. I'll warn you just once. Now get out of bed."

Kearns got up. His knees were weak, and he

could barely stand, and his mind was blank from panic.

"Get dressed," ordered Pejack.

Owen fumbled around.

"I can't find my clothes," he said.

"Help him," Pejack told Bianco.

Gantzel let a hand move over Cleo's body, and she coiled and straightened as quick as a snake and went for his eyes.

"Gantzel!" said Pejack.

He pinioned her arms again.

"She's a wildcat," said Gantzel.

"Let her go," said Bianco. "I can see you in the dark." His voice held a warning.

"Let her go," said Pejack.

Gantzel let go of Cleo, and she rubbed at her wrists, then moved to the bed and slipped on a robe.

"I'm dressed," said Owen.

He stood ready, a wilted figure in the dark, and Cleo felt sick. He was not being much of a man.

"What do you want from him?" she asked.

"Let's go," said Pejack.

"The girl, too?" said Bianco.

"No," said Pejack.

"I'll stay with her," said Gantzel.

"Bianco will stay with her," said Pejack.

"Why not me?" said Gantzel.

"Because you asked to," said Pejack.

"Never volunteer," said Bianco.

And he laughed.

"What are you after?" insisted Cleo.

"The gold," said Owen. "They think I can take them into the mill."

"You can, smart man," said Pejack.

He prodded Owen to go ahead of him, and Gantzel followed them out the door.

"Save some for me," Gantzel told Bianco.

"Someday I'll put my knife in you," said Bianco.

He closed the door after the gunman and turned to Cleo. "Get dressed," he told her. "You go with us."

"Get dressed in front of you?"

"It's dark."

"But you can see in the dark. Turn around."

He shrugged, and she smiled at him.

"We are both Mexican," she pointed out.

"I can't help you," he told her. "Dress warmly, for you won't be coming back."

Outside the cabin, Pejack told Owen to stop.

"Where's Hall?" Pejack asked.

"He's sleeping in his office," said Owen.

"We'll detour around the office," said Pejack. "You lead, we'll follow. Act like you're just going about your business, checking to see that everything is ready for morning."

"You know about the shipment?"

"We know, and I'll know if you try to give us away. How many guards are at the mill?"

"Two. Hall posts two men the night before a shipment."

"Where's Fender?"

"I don't know. Sleeping probably. He has to escort the shipment, and they don't stop once they get started."

"You tell the guards it's okay. We're just checking."

"They'll know something's wrong. They won't recognize you."

"Once we get close enough to be recognized, it'll be all over," said Pejack. "Make a bad move, and you and your wife will both regret it."

They began walking uphill toward the mill.

The mill was built in steps down the slope of the mountain. The room they wanted was on the lower level of the mill, and when they drew near, they could see a man sitting beside the door.

"The wagon's not here yet," said Gantzel.

"Shut up," said Pejack.

He prodded Owen's back with his revolver to remind him, then slipped the gun into the holster. The guard stood up and pointed his rifle at them.

"Stop right there," said the guard.

"It's only me," said Owen. "How's everything?"

"Fine, Mr. Kearns. I didn't expect to see you here tonight."

The guard lowered his rifle.

"Just checking," said Owen.

Pejack hurried Owen forward, and they came up on the guard before the man realized anything was wrong.

"Who's that with you?" began the guard.

Gantzel jammed a gun in the man's ribs.

"Quiet now," said Pejack.

The guard looked down at the gun, and Pejack reached out and took his rifle.

"Open the door," Pejack told Owen.

"It's locked," said Owen.

"Where's the key?"

"It's locked from the inside," said Owen. "The other guard has the key."

"Tell him to open up," said Pejack.

Owen knocked on the door, but there was no answer. They could hear something from down the mountain, a creaking sound, and then the snort of a horse.

"Wagon's coming," said Gantzel.

"Hurry up," said Pejack to Kearns.

Owen knocked again, harder, and they heard the sound of feet inside.

"It's Owen Kearns," said Owen. "Are you asleep in there?"

A key rattled in the lock, and as they heard the lock click, Pejack hurled himself at the door. The door flew inward, knocking the man inside off balance, and Pejack was on him. The guard was covered, but he had already started reaching for his handgun, and Pejack pistol-whipped him across the side of the head. The guard fell and lay moaning, while Gantzel hustled the other two inside. Owen stood looking down at the fallen man. Blood had started running out of his mouth and ears.

"You killed him," said the first guard.

"Don't talk, listen," said Pejack. "We're going to relieve you of the bullion. You're going to carry it out and load it on a wagon."

"You won't get far," said the guard.

"And you won't live long if you don't shut up," said Gantzel.

"Kearns," said Pejack. "Open the safe."

Kearns looked at Pejack and wet his lips with his tongue. He nodded and looked about him as if in a daze.

The mill room was warmed by the banked fires of the smelter. A wire cage from ceiling to floor surrounded the safe, a large, solid block of steel in one corner of the room. A man could walk into the safe, it was so large.

"Come on, come on," said Pejack.

"I need the keys to the cage," said Owen.

Pejack turned the man on the floor over and rummaged through his pockets.

"No keys," he said, straightening.

They could hear the wagon pull up outside.

"We should have the safe open already," said Gantzel.

He was nervous, and his voice sounded more

like a hiss than a man's voice. Pejack looked at the first guard.

"Brooks Hall keeps the only key," said the guard.

Pejack crossed to a workbench and picked up a steel bar. He went to the door in the cage and put the bar under the lock and snapped it off with vicious leverage.

Johnny stepped inside the mill room, saw the man on the floor, and then glanced at Pejack.

"He's all right," said Pejack. "Keep a watch at the door while we get the safe open. Owen!"

Owen walked into the cage and approached the safe.

"Don't say you don't know the combination," warned Pejack.

Owen rubbed his hands on his pants and then held them out toward the dials. There was a numbered dial on each of the double doors, and Owen's hands shook as he reached for one of them.

Johnny, standing outside, saw a man coming swiftly up the mountain. It was Goodhard.

"Any trouble?" asked Goodhard.

Johnny shook his head and went inside with Goodhard. He found a pile of gunnysacks and took an armful back outside and began muffling the wheels while the others waited for the safe to get open.

Kearns was sweating. He wiped at his face and tried again and failed.

"What's the matter?" asked Pejack impatiently.

"Maybe Hall changed the combination," said Owen, his voice breaking.

"He'd better not have," said Pejack. "I'll give you ten seconds."

Owen took a deep breath and began again.

Goodhard looked at his watch. They were running late. A morning patrol was due by in twenty minutes, and they had to have the gold loaded and be gone before then.

The tumblers fell into place on the first lock, and Owen drew another breath and reached for the second dial.

The men in the rough-beamed, low-ceilinged room waited, frozen in intense concentration as they all watched Kearns.

Pejack heard the last tumbler click, and he pushed Owen aside and turned the handles on the doors. The doors swung open, and they saw the gold. It was a sight to take away their breath. Large gold bars were stacked neatly like cordwood inside the vault. There were six bars, and the metal gleamed brightly, polished and alive. The gold had a fresh-minted, untouched look, and Pejack could feel his heart almost stop from excitement. He had never dreamed there would be so much of it.

"Get busy," he told the others.

The men filed into the wire cage, and Gantzel was first. He tried to lift a bar of gold, looked surprised, and took a firmer grip. It was all he could do to move one bar.

"Each bar weighs at least seventy-five pounds," said Pejack. "Don't let one fall against another with your fingers between them. The dead weight of two bars would crush your hand."

Gantzel began carrying the first bar out to the wagon. The guard picked up one and followed, and Goodhard took his turn.

"You too," Pejack told Owen.

Owen could just barely walk under the weight, and he held the bar clear down by his knees.

Johnny stood in the wagon and arranged the weight over the axles.

Owen was alone at the wagon for a moment with Johnny.

"Where's Cleo?" whispered Johnny.

Owen looked up in surprise.

"At the house," he replied.

"Is Bianco guarding her?"

"I don't know his name," said Owen.

Johnny made a motion to be silent as Goodhard came out, and Owen returned to the mill.

"Where's Toomey?" asked Johnny.

"You'll find out," said Goodhard.

"I'm beginning not to like you very much," said Johnny.

"In your hat," said Goodhard.

Johnny grabbed the man's shirt and pulled him forward.

"If I find out you finished that man at the corral, I'll do the same for you," he said.

He pushed Goodhard away, and Goodhard spat on the ground to show how frightened he was, then he went back inside.

"That's all," said Pejack. "The wagon's got to be gone before the patrol comes by. Let's go. Gantzel, you know what to do."

They left, and Gantzel closed the door behind them. "Turn around," said Gantzel.

The remaining guard looked at his companion, still lying soundless on the floor.

"Please," said the guard, turning. "I've got three kids back home."

Gantzel drew his gun and reversed it like a club.

Owen Kearns was made to get up on the wagon seat beside Johnny, and Goodhard climbed into the wagon bed behind them.

"I'll walk ahead," said Pejack. "If we run into anybody, let me take care of them."

Pejack walked downhill purposefully, as if he belonged, and Johnny clucked, and the horses strained, and the wagon started. Johnny set the brake and used it to hold the wagon from catching up to the horses on the down slope.

"Where to?" he asked Goodhard.

"Patience. The thing is not to be seen."

"What about Cleo?" said Owen. "What have you done with her?"

"She'll be there waiting," said Goodhard.

The wagon moved quietly enough, but the harness jingled, and the men in the wagon sat tensely, staring off into the dark, expecting to be challenged at any moment.

They detoured around Hall's office once more and approached Lucky from the top of the street. Johnny did not like it. Any drunk or light sleeper might spot them. It was after one a.m., but that was no guarantee everybody was sleeping.

Pejack did not lead them down the street. He ducked behind the first tent building, and Johnny guided the team in behind the large tent and reined in behind Harry Stiles's saloon—and Johnny began to understand.

Goodhard pulled the tarp off the gold bars, and Pejack let down the tailgate.

"Let's go," said Pejack. "Move fast."

Johnny and Owen got down as Harry Stiles came out of the rear of the saloon. He tied the flap back, and the men started carrying the gold inside while Goodhard stood guard in the street.

When Johnny carried his bar of gold inside, he did not see the others. There were no lamps lit, and it looked like they had just vanished in the dark. Then he heard voices, and he saw a faint glow of light from the ground behind an old wood stove in the kitchen. He walked forward and saw dirt steps leading down, just as Pejack came up them.

"Down there," said Pejack. "We've got minutes to unload and reload."

Pejack went outside, and Johnny walked down the steps into a cellar beneath the saloon. It was a small room and crowded. Toomey was there, working at a miniature smelter. He was stripped to the waist, and sweat ran off his face and shoulders. Bianco and Cleo were there too, and Bianco went up the steps to help unload as Owen staggered down with a bar.

"Owen," said Cleo.

She went to him, and he put the gold ingot down, and they embraced. She paid no notice to Johnny.

Johnny crossed to Toomey to see what he was doing and found him laboring over a gold bar. Toomey looked up and watched the expression on Johnny's face. Johnny saw a half-dozen gold bars exactly like those stolen from the mill, and he whistled softly.

"What do you think?" asked Toomey. "Can you see any difference?"

"No," said Johnny. "Where'd they come from?"

"I made them," said Toomey with obvious pride.

He picked up a finished ingot and took it to the pile of real ingots and set it beside one of them.

He stood studying the two with infinite care, and Johnny looked, too.

"Color's perfect," said Toomey. "The color is the first thing that gives a gold brick away."

"Gold is gold to me," said Johnny.

"It is to most people, but not to an expert. You can tell the exact source of gold. Did you know that? You can tell what county, what mine it came from. I used high-grade gold from Hall's own mine to coat these bricks. It's got a little silver and some copper in it still. No gold coming from the mill is pure twenty-four-carat gold. This runs about thirty-three fine. Pure gold is a soft yellow, but copper gives it an orange color and silver a pale lemon cast. If I didn't use the exact same ingredients from Hall's mill, he'd be able to tell right off."

Toomey turned one of the real ingots over and pointed to a small mark.

"Hall's gold mark," said Toomey.

There was the same mark, the initials "BLH" in a circle on the gold bricks.

"Brooks's Lucky Hall," said Toomey. "That's what it stands for."

"Better not get the two mixed up," said Johnny.

Toomey carried the false ingot back to where the others lay.

"How many did you get?" asked Toomey.

"Six ingots," said Johnny.

"That's over two hundred thousand dollars,"

said Toomey. "Better than we counted on. Brooks has got himself a good thing."

Stiles came down with the last of the bullion, and after he put it down, he turned to Johnny.

"Pejack wants to see you," said Stiles.

Johnny nodded and climbed the stairs, and Stiles stayed behind to watch Owen and Cleo.

Pejack was waiting in the kitchen, and he offered Johnny a cigar. They lit up, and Pejack got right to it.

"Your job is to get as much distance as possible out of that team. Draw Hall's men the hell-and-gone away from here so we can take off in the opposite direction. When you come back, we'll take mules and pack over the pass. Bianco knows a way nobody can follow, and before you go, he'll tell you how to follow."

"How do I know he'll tell me the right way?"

"You don't."

Johnny pushed his hat back on his head and stood looking down at Pejack.

"You made a promise about the girl and Kearns," said Johnny.

"I'll keep my promise," said Pejack.

"I mean to see you do," said Johnny.

They had the wagon reloaded in minutes, and Johnny finished his cigar in the kitchen while he waited for Bianco. Harry Stiles sidled up to him, mopping his brow and puffing.

"Didn't think I'd be sweating on such a cold

night," said Harry. "How'd you get into this deal?"

Johnny shrugged.

"How'd you?" he asked.

"I'd been buying high-grade from the miners," said Stiles. "Had the smelter set up down there. It used to be Pejack's root cellar, and he caught on to me quick. I'd buy high-grade for twenty dollars an ounce to sell later at twenty-five. Pejack said either come in or talk to Hall. I came in."

They were silent for a moment.

"Are you going with them?" asked Johnny.

"Pejack isn't about to leave me behind to talk," said Stiles. "We had a little conversation once ourselves. I hope you'll forget about that."

Johnny thought back and remembered that Stiles had been anxious to get away. It meant that Harry was not too happy with the deal.

"I've already forgotten," said Johnny.

Pejack and Bianco came up out of the cellar.

"Ready?" said Pejack.

"Yep," said Johnny.

"Let's go."

They filed outside, and Johnny stood by the wagon. They were all there now, Goodhard, Gantzel, Bianco, Pejack, and Stiles; everybody but Toomey and the Kearnses, and Johnny figured he had one friend among them, and he was not too sure of that. Harry Stiles could be worked on, and Bianco was a question mark. The others could be written off. If it came to trouble, there was only Toomey, and Johnny could not be sure of him.

"Johnny, listen carefully," said Pejack. "When you get the wagon back on the street, we'll brush out the tracks leading in here. As you pass the corrals, Goodhard will let the stock out, so they'll have to waste time rounding up horses. Once you hit open country, get cracking. If you're caught, think twice before you give us away. Bianco says you knew Cleo sometime back, and if you want to see her alive, don't tell any tales."

"I want a gun and a horse," said Johnny.

"Give him a gun," said Pejack.

Goodhard handed over the rifle he had taken from the guard at the corral.

"What about the horse?" asked Johnny.

"Give him a horse," said Bianco. "If he gets caught, he might not be able to keep from talking."

"All right," said Pejack. "Goodhard, go saddle a horse and meet him on the road below town."

Goodhard left.

"Where do I go if I make it back?" asked Johnny.

"You've seen the high peaks above town?" said Bianco.

"Yes."

"There's an easy pass to the right of the highest

peak. If they follow, they'll think we went that way because there is no other pass. To the left are sheer rock walls."

"But you know a way?"

"The Indians go back and forth there. Climb the mountain until you see a needle of rock. Guide for it until you can see the town at your back, the needle before, and to the north, the great peak that always has snow. There you turn south one mile exactly, then turn west until you come against the stone face of the mountain. If you have done right, you will find a way to scale the cliff."

"And if I don't find it?"

"*Quién sabe*?"

"That's enough talk," said Pejack.

Johnny got up on the seat and let off the brake. He guided the team in a wide circle back to the street and picked up his tracks again. The others erased the detour sign with pine boughs and disappeared back into the saloon. Bianco, Pejack, and Gantzel went down the steps into the cellar, and Stiles closed the trap door and moved the coal stove back on top of it. He took a deep breath, then went into the darkened saloon and poured himself a big drink.

Johnny sat hunched on the wagon, steering it down Lucky's short street. There were no lights in the tents, and even the Golden Ram was dark. A dog raised its head, sniffed the air, and watched the horses plod by. Men turned in their sleep at the sound of harness and cursed, thinking surely it could not be time to rise. They had only just gotten to sleep.

The wagon passed through town safely, and Johnny saw Goodhard waiting in the road, holding a saddle horse.

"I picked you a good one," said Goodhard.

"Tie him on back," said Johnny.

Goodhard walked the horse around back then came to Johnny again.

"How much of a cut is Pejack giving you?" said Goodhard.

"Enough," said Johnny.

"Whatever it is, it's too much," said Goodhard. "When we began, there was only Pejack and Bianco and me. Now there's you and Toomey and Stiles to split with. You once said all you wanted was to leave Lucky. You've got the chance now. Take it. When that team plays out, get on the horse and keep going."

"I guess not," said Johnny. "I've got some unfinished business."

"The girl? I'll treat her good. Leave her to me."

"No," said Johnny. "You're my business."

He flicked the reins and started the team again, and when he was out of sight, he stopped and got down and went back to look at the horse. It was a stump-sucker, an aged mare that would blow out after a mile of running. Johnny checked the reins and found that they would come free after a short time. Johnny retied the knot and got back up on the seat. The stars said that it was still three hours before dawn, and Johnny got the team moving. Three hours was not time enough to do all that had to be done.

13

Goodhard came down the steps into the cellar.

"Did you let the stock out?" asked Pejack.

"Yeah."

"I hope you scattered them good."

"I did," said Goodhard.

It was so crowded that Pejack did not notice that Goodhard was carrying a bottle of whiskey.

Gantzel, Bianco, and Toomey were playing cards. Owen and Cleo sat together on a box watching the men. There was hardly room to turn around in, and the air was acrid and the temperature sweltering from the smelting that Toomey had been doing.

The only ventilation in the room was a stovepipe in the ceiling that connected to the stove in Stiles's kitchen. Goodhard stole drinks out of the bottle whenever Pejack wasn't looking. He leaned against the dirt wall and nipped and studied Cleo, who wore a riding outfit—boots, split skirt, blouse, and broad-brimmed hat. The top button of the blouse was unbuttoned, and Cleo saw the man studying her. He was an ugly, gross man, and the thought of him sickened her.

"Maybe we should start now," said Goodhard. "I don't like this waiting."

"We're safe," said Bianco.

"Goodhard's right," said Gantzel. "We're sitting ducks down here."

"They might discover we tricked them," said Goodhard. "If Hall cuts into those bricks, he'll tear Lucky apart looking for us."

"He won't," said Toomey. "I could sell one of those bricks to any bank in Denver. They're a work of art."

"We stay here," said Pejack. "The idea is to draw Hall away from town. That's the plan, and we'll stick to it. Better try to get some rest."

"I'm too wound up to sleep," said Gantzel.

"Me, too," said Goodhard.

"You'll need strength to scale the cliffs," said Bianco. "Better try to sleep."

"Maybe we could have some fun," said Goodhard, ignoring Bianco.

He was looking at Cleo.

She drew nearer Owen, and Pejack glanced at Goodhard.

"Where'd you get that bottle?" said Pejack.

"Upstairs."

"Get rid of it."

Goodhard thought about it. He took another pull, and Pejack stood up.

"Let him have his fun," said Gantzel.

"I'm giving the orders," said Pejack.

Toomey watched carefully. Gantzel and Goodhard were together. Pejack was in the middle.

Bianco sat relaxed and unconcerned. It was between Pejack and the other two.

"We're stuck here for a hard, long day," said Pejack. "If we start drinking, there's going to be trouble. There'll be men in and out of the saloon above, and if they hear us, we're trapped. I say no booze."

Goodhard looked at Gantzel, and the gunman smiled.

"Hell," said Gantzel, "There's time to sleep. I'm for funning. Nobody's going to be coming into the saloon this early."

"It's been a long time since we saw a woman," put in Goodhard.

"No!" said Pejack.

"Why not?" asked Gantzel reasonably.

Toomey knew that if they got started, they would not stop, and Pejack was losing control.

"Use your head," said Pejack. "Why take chances?"

Gantzel and Goodhard were both staring at Cleo.

Toomey got up and walked toward the bullion.

"There's something we haven't talked about," said Toomey. "Isn't anybody interested in how much gold we got?"

His words caused Gantzel to pause.

"How much?" asked Gantzel.

"Twice what we figured," said Toomey. "Double shares, but that causes a problem. It's going to be harder to freight over the mountain. How we going to do it, Bianco?"

Bianco got up and tried to heft a gold bar.

"*Por Dios*, it's heavy," said Bianco. "Maybe we leave some behind?"

"You lazy Mex," said Gantzel. "I'm not leaving an ounce."

"We'll have to consider," said Bianco.

They fell to arguing on how they would get all that weight over the cliffs, and Toomey breathed easier.

Goodhard climbed up the steps after another bottle and would not listen when Pejack told him to come back. Toomey sat down by Cleo and Owen.

"Do you think he can hold them?" asked Owen, indicating Pejack.

"My grandpappy used to say, 'In war, a fortress that parleys is half-taken,' " said Toomey.

Cleo shuddered.

"Bianco's harder than the rest," she said. "I'm more afraid of him than the others."

"He's got a sense of humor," said Toomey. "He can't be all bad."

Owen started to speak, but Cleo put her hand on his arm, and Owen was silent. The balance was shifting between the thieves, and it was best for them to stay out of it.

"Do you think we could get something to eat?" asked Cleo aloud.

“Sure,” said Goodhard, grinning. “You just tell me when you want anything.”

As dawn approached, the men in the cellar grew watchful. They waited for sounds of alarm from whoever would discover the theft. There was sure to be hell to pay, but if everything went well, the town would not be searched.

“So far, so good, eh, Gantzel?” said Goodhard.

“Yeah.”

“Terrell should be far away,” said Bianco. “It will be hours before they find the wagon, hours coming back. They’ll comb the land where they find the wagon, looking for us.”

“They don’t know who we are,” said Gantzel. “Pejack, Bianco, and me are safe. They’ll be looking for Terrell and Toomey.”

“Johnny will make it,” said Toomey.

“They’ll know there were others,” said Bianco. “And they’ll search for the Kearnses too.”

“We’re rich,” said Goodhard, looking at the pile of ingots. “How much do you figure each share comes to?”

“We’ll divide the gold in Mexico,” said Pejack. “You can forget about it until we get there.”

Goodhard sat down by the bullion and let his hand rest on one of the bars. His face was red from whiskey, and he stroked the gold fondly.

“Beautiful,” said Goodhard.

“Listen!” said Bianco.

They froze in silence, and at first, they did not hear anything; then someone stamped on the floor overhead.

"That's Stiles's signal," said Pejack. "He's warning us to be quiet."

They could hear shouts from far away, and then the sound of a gun, and the men in the cellar looked at one another and were silent. All they could do now was wait.

Brooks Hall was dressed and at his desk when he heard the first warning. Someone in town fired a gun. He went to the door, opened it, and looked down the hill to see men running toward the corral. He could see that the corral gate was hanging open and all the stock was out. He ran downhill to the corral.

Hall found a group of men crowded around a dead man, and they parted to let him through. Fender was already there, kneeling over the corpse. Fender glanced up at Brooks Hall.

"It's Hastings," said Fender. "He was on guard. They tied him up, and then they must have decided to kill him. Broke his skull."

"Who did it?" asked Hall. "How many?"

"Don't know," said Fender. "This crowd has already stamped out the tracks."

"Find out how many saddles are gone," said Hall. "Get horses and pick some men. I want the people who did this."

"I've already got men out after the horses," said Fender.

Hall turned and strode off as some of the horses were being driven down the main street.

A man who was obviously a mule skinner came running toward Hall.

"There's a wagon missing, Mr. Hall," he shouted.

Hall stopped short. He looked at the mule skinner, then his eyes went up the hill toward the mill.

"Fender!" said Hall.

His voice was like the crack of a whip.

Fender came running.

"The mill," said Hall.

They ran, with the crowd at their heels, and Hall was the first one there. He tried the door and found it locked.

"The outside guard's gone," said Fender.

They broke the door down and spilled into the smelting room. Three men lay on the floor. The two guards and the patrol that Gantzel had stayed behind to intercept. All three were dead, their skulls crushed.

"Poor Charley," said a miner. "He had three kids."

Hall went to stand in the doorway of the bullion room.

The safe doors stood open.

"We'll get 'em," said Fender, talking to Hall.

"You had better."

Fender knew he was in trouble, but he was smart enough to keep quiet now.

"Any ideas?" said Hall.

"They can't be traveling fast. That's a heavy load."

"But they could have left early in the night," said Hall.

"Not before midnight. I checked here myself sometime after eleven."

"That's six hours ago. Saddle a horse for me," said Hall. "I'm going with you."

Hall went outside and strode to the house. He threw open the front door, crossed to the bedroom, and kicked the door. The lock flew off as the door banged open, and Hall barely looked inside. He knew Cleo and Owen would not be there. He was going out again when Sing Lee came into the living room.

"Want blekfast now, Mr. Hall?" said Sing Lee.

Brooks did not hear him, and Sing Lee sighed and looked at the broken and splintered door in wonder. He did not understand Americans.

Fender brought Hall's horse as soon as it was saddled. Hall came out of his office dressed in black knee-length boots, and he had a gun strapped on under his coat. He mounted and looked at Fender.

"Kearns and that whore are gone," said Hall.

"You said she had something in mind coming here," pointed out Fender.

"I never would have guessed it was this," said Hall. "It's not Kearns's dish of tea."

"Why not? He's stolen before."

"Embezzlement, not murder. I can't see Cleo in it either. It's coarse, not like a woman."

"She isn't exactly a lily."

"They'd need help. Who else is missing?"

"I haven't seen that big cowboy Terrell this morning," said Fender. "Nobody else has either, and Goodhard's gone."

"Of course," said Hall, and he smiled. "No wonder Terrell turned down that job."

"What job?"

"Never mind."

Hall rode to the corral where other men were getting ready. Two dozen riders were saddling horses, and they were all armed.

"We'll follow the wagon as far as the forks," Hall said to Fender. "When we see which way they've gone, we'll start cutting across country to make up time. I want everybody to keep their eyes open."

"Think they'll try to bury it?"

"Could be. It'll be hard to go anywhere and peddle that much gold. They've got to have some plan to get rid of it. That may take time."

"We'll catch them," said Fender. "If they've

buried the gold, I'll make them talk. I can make anybody talk."

"I'm sure you can," said Hall.

The posse moved out in a long column, and the miners watched them go, then went to the saloons to talk about it. There would be little work done in Lucky that day.

14

The wagon swung into a canyon, and Johnny, sitting up high on the box, felt the rear axletree and bolster skid as the rear of the wagon fish-tailed on the corner. A cloud of dust obscured his rear view, and he did not bother to look back. He was driving the team hard, and the six-horse team could pull the wagon at a fair clip. He sat right behind the off, or right-wheel, horse, and he used the whip and a pocketful of pebbles to keep them running. His eyes sought out the road ahead, then switched back to horses and harness. At this speed, a broken strap or toggle meant disaster.

On the mountain trail down, the wagon had bounced and jarred over rock-strewn grades. In the basins, the wheels cut deeply, churning up itchy alkali, and the sweat-covered horses and Johnny were caked with white powder and dust.

At the forks, he turned south along the foothills road beside the desert. The lead horse was strong and kept the others tearing, and Johnny knew he could get forty miles out of them with a rest and water. He nooned the team at dawn, driving them into a shallow stream, and he got down and waded in the water and unhooked the two toggles between the leaders, swings, and wheelers so the horses could drink.

He splashed water on his face and drank, then went back and got the rifle from the box and checked it.

The rifle was an old Henry Flat repeater, heavy but a good gun, and Johnny threw it to his shoulder to get its feel, then he put it back and hitched up again.

The team pulled the ore wagon out of the stream bed, up the steep-cut bank, wild-eyed and straining, then they were running on the flat once more. At the top of the first good rise, Johnny pulled on the six reins and whoaed the team. He stood up and looked back. He could see a good distance. The sun was full and hot. The morning shadows were gone and the land lay exposed. There was no dust in the air on the road behind him, and Johnny figured he had another hour. They would have started after him at dawn, and he wanted to be nowhere near the wagon when they caught up to it.

He sat down and cracked the whip.

"Hi-yi! G'long! Up there!"

The horses were getting tired, but they went.

"Go there, you red!"

He pushed as hard as he could, a killing pace, and when he noticed the off-swing horse stumble, he eased up. That one had gone lame, and Johnny knew they were all done.

The sun was high, and Johnny walked the team, watching for a likely place to leave them.

Ahead lay a long grade, gradual but with enough slope to keep the wagon rolling, and Johnny set the brake lever at half and tied the reins to it. He climbed into the box of the wagon and threw the tarp aside, revealing the gold bricks.

Johnny hefted each brick over the side of the wagon and dropped them one by one into the short clump grass. Then he pulled the saddle horse close, untied the reins, and climbed on and sat watching the wagon go on without him. The wagon would keep rolling on the downgrade, pushing the horses ahead of it for a mile or two.

He rode back and covered each gold brick but one with sand, as if he were trying to hide them, and then he remounted, taking the remaining brick, and rode west into the mountains at an easy lope. There was no use running the horse until he had to.

Hall led the posse, with Fender close behind, and the other men were strung out for a mile on their less hardy ponies.

Hall held up a hand in the creek bed, and the others splashed down and crowded around.

"He stopped here," said Fender.

"Not for long," said Hall.

Brooks Hall goaded his horse out of the stream and up the cut bank without more palaver, and the others crashed up behind, clods flying from hoofs. The sound of twenty-six horses running shook the earth and reverberated off the low hills.

They stopped again where Johnny had looked back from the rise, but they could not see the wagon, and on they thundered.

"He's killing the horses," said a man.

"Wouldn't you?" answered another.

Fender rode up beside Hall and indicated that they should stop, and Brooks reined back, almost throwing his horse.

"What is it?" asked Hall.

"They slowed here," said Fender. "They're not running the team."

Brooks looked at the tracks of the wagon and team in the road and nodded, and the posse went on at a slower pace. They found the wagon at the bottom of the grade, one horse down in harness, and Fender climbed into the wagon. He threw the tarp out, and the wagon bed lay empty.

"Scatter out on both sides of the road," ordered Hall. "Look for their tracks."

They soon discovered no one had ridden on ahead, and they began working the back trail. Men rode on both sides of the rutted trail, watching for sign.

"Something I don't understand," said Mick.

"What?" asked Hall.

"I've been studying their tracks all the way, a six-horse team and a spare horse. Just one. If they're cutting across country, somebody's walking."

"Maybe there's just one of them."

"Could be," said Mick.

A cowboy yelled, and everybody rode toward him. Hall got there in time to see the man pulling and tugging at a bright gold bar sticking up out of the sand.

He got down, pushed the man aside, and brushed the sand away.

"Somebody bring up the wagon," said Fender.

A couple of riders went off for the wagon, and Mick got down to stand over Hall, who was studying the gold bar.

"That's one," said Hall, his fingers touching the initials on the bullion. "There're five more. Let's find them."

The men piled off and began digging in the sand eagerly.

Fender found Johnny's trail and rode out west a ways and came back.

"Just one man," he told Hall. "There's something wrong in it."

"We'll get him before night," said Brooks.

"There's still something I don't like about it," repeated Fender.

They found all but one ingot, and Hall stood looking west toward the mountains.

"There's a man out there with something that belongs to me," Hall told them. "I want him alive if he'll let us take him that way. I'm going to hang him in Lucky."

They got up, and Fender sent a half-dozen of his best with the wagon back toward Lucky, and the others rode into the mountains.

Johnny sat his horse on the second ridge. He could see the posse ten miles away, two thousand feet below. They looked like angry ants as they crawled single file through the dark spots that would be scrub juniper brush. He turned his horse and rode away minus the gold bar. It had been a burden. Someday, someone would find it hidden in the cleft rocks, and they would think they were rich—for a little while.

Johnny had not taken any great pains to cover his trail, but now he kept to hard ground and looked for ways to lose those following. He did not want them to know when he turned back north.

He got down and led his horse up steep hillsides and through timber. Noon came and went, and Johnny reached the high country. He found a hillside of sloping rock, and here he turned north again toward Lucky. His horse left no sign, and Johnny began to hurry him. He wanted to be at the cliffs above Lucky before dark.

Fender and Hall were far ahead of the others. Tired horses were strung out for miles behind them, but Hall would not call a rest.

Fender got down from time to time to search for Johnny's trail and point out a broken twig or clump of grass to show which way to go, and they pushed on. They found where Johnny had stood watching them from the second ridge.

"Let's go," said Hall.

"The horses can't keep this up," said Fender.

"We can't wait. He's got a fresh horse. If we don't get him before dark, we'll never catch him."

"He's made it too easy," said Fender. "Let's think on it a minute."

"Too easy?"

"The wagon deserted, the bullion next to the road hardly buried, the easy trail to here. He's leading us on," said Mick.

Brooks Hall got out a cigar, lit it, and puffed slowly. He began to feel something new.

"Just one man," pointed out Mick. "Where are the others? We caught the wagon easy. The gold was buried as if it was meant to be found. I think we've been suckered somehow."

"But how?"

They stared at each other, but there was no answer.

When the others began straggling onto the hilltop, Hall sent one of them back to catch the wagon and take another look at the gold.

The rest of them went on trailing the lone man. He would have answers, and he would talk, but they lost the trail often now.

"He's trying," said Mick Fender.

"It looks like you were right," agreed Hall.

When they lost the trail completely, Hall did not waste time looking for it. He turned the tired men north, and they pushed on toward Lucky. It was after dark when they got back, and some of them rode double, leaving lame horses in the mountains to forage for themselves.

Hall went directly to the mill and stood looking at the gold bricks.

"Lead," said a mill hand. "Good job. Real thing on the outside, but not worth a jitney."

"They had to do it right here," he told Fender. "They had to have my gold to fool me, and they had to know my mark."

"Kearns," guessed Fender. "He's the only one."

"I don't think so," said Hall.

"He knew the mark. He could have gotten hold of your gold easy and had the bricks made in Santa Fe."

"Maybe, but I don't believe it. It's too bold for Owen."

They walked outside and stood looking down at Lucky.

"Find that Toomey for me," said Hall at last.

"He's only been here two, three days," said Fender.

"Find him," ordered Hall.

He went to his office to wait, and an hour later, when Fender opened the door, Brooks already knew.

"He's gone," said Fender.

"I think I've figured it out," said Hall. "Who's a good suspect for high-grading?"

"Any of a hundred men."

"Then it shouldn't be hard to pick out one that'll talk."

"Where'll that get us?"

"They had to smelt the ore down," said Hall.

"And that's where we'll find the gold?"

"If we're not too late."

"You think it's still in Lucky?"

"It could be halfway to Mexico by now. The smelter will be deserted, but it's a starting point. Send some men toward the pass and have them look for sign of a pack train."

15

Bianco slept peacefully. He had a way of relaxing that infuriated Gantzel, and the gunman swung his foot and nudged the Mexican.

"Hey, Bianco, how can you sleep?"

Bianco opened his eyes to slits.

Goodhard and Gantzel exchanged smiles, and Gantzel nudged Bianco again with his foot.

"Wake up," said Gantzel. "It's time to take a siesta."

Bianco came up like a coiled spring before Gantzel could have his laugh, and the gunman found himself looking at the razor-sharp point of a knife.

Bianco held the knife point, gently touching Gantzel's lower lip.

"Keep your tongue and your feet to yourself," warned Bianco.

"Bianco!" said Pejack. "Quiet, all of you. They can hear."

Everybody glanced overhead at the rafters supporting the floor of Harry Stiles's saloon. The sound of miners moving to and fro came easily to their ears, as it had all day.

"Next time I'll carve you," said Bianco.

Bianco put the knife away and turned his back on Gantzel. He could use a knife better than most men could use a gun, and Gantzel kept his tongue. Owen sat slump-shouldered beside Cleo. Toomey, Pejack, and Goodhard were playing cards.

"That's three thousand you owe me," said Toomey to Goodhard.

Goodhard threw his hand in as Toomey toted up the last bet on a piece of paper.

"Don't you ever lose?" asked Goodhard.

"A run of luck," said Toomey.

"Luck or something else."

"Say that again," said Toomey, stiffening.

"What time is it?" asked Goodhard, changing the subject.

"Nine p.m.," said Pejack.

"I wish we knew what was going on upstairs," said Goodhard.

"Want to quit?" asked Toomey.

"When I'm stuck three thousand?" said Goodhard. "Deal."

"We'll pull out as soon as Stiles signals it's quiet," said Pejack.

Owen Kearns had had time to get over his initial fear only to find a new one. Every time one of the men looked at Cleo or came near her, he shook. Owen knew he would have to make the attempt to protect her, but he was so weak-willed that he did not know what he could do if someone did molest her. He would try, but he was afraid.

"Cold?" he asked Cleo.

"No, not very," she said.

It was cool in the cellar now, and they were both stiff from sitting so long.

"Want my coat?" he asked.

"No, you keep it."

"I'm sorry I got you into this."

"It's not your fault."

"They'll let us go when they're in the clear," he said.

"Yes," she answered.

But neither of them believed it.

Johnny passed around Lucky in the late afternoon. He could see the town below him, and he stopped to study it. Everything looked peaceful, and nobody was moving around much. The buildings were tiny from that distance, but he could make them out. No smoke came from the chimneys of the mill. Here and there, smoke drifted up from a stovepipe stuck through a canvas roof, and Johnny could see smoke rising from Harry Stiles's saloon. That meant they had not left yet, and Johnny paused to consider.

He looked ahead to the pass where the sheer cliffs rose, gun-metal gray against the sky. Puffs of clouds drifted over the high mountains toward him, and Johnny gauged their speed. There was a storm coming, and Pejack evidently intended to scale the cliffs at night. Johnny got down off his horse and found a place to wait out the daylight. When it was dark, Johnny walked, leading his horse down, and he worked his way closer and closer to town.

It was late when the last man had his last drink in Stiles's saloon. Harry walked the man to the door, said goodnight, and was drawing the canvas flap closed to tie it shut when Mick Fender and Brooks Hall and a crowd of men loomed out of the dark and came toward him. Stiles froze in the doorway.

Fender pushed Harry backward into the saloon as the men walked purposefully inside. They ranged in a quiet circle around Stiles, and Harry glanced from one to another of them. He could not bring himself to meet Hall's gaze, and his eyes came back to rest uneasily on Mick Fender.

"What's this about?" asked Harry.

"We didn't come for a drink," said Fender.

Harry did not move.

"Where's the gold?" asked Hall.

"What gold?"

Fender hit Harry, and he fell where he stood. He lay in the sawdust on the floor a long second, then shook his head and tried to rise.

"The gold," said Hall.

"I don't know," said Harry.

Fender kicked Harry in the chest, and they could hear bone snap.

"That's enough," said Hall, and he turned to the others. "Take this place apart."

Some of them went to the bar and began looking in barrels and boxes. Others took the kitchen. They split open sacks of flour and overturned the larder. One man even looked inside the woodstove oven and burned his hand on the hot handle, but they did not find anything.

"Put him in a chair," said Hall.

One of the men propped Harry up in a Hitchcock chair and held him upright by the hair. Fender slapped Harry's face until he came around.

"Can you hear me?" asked Fender.

Harry tried to nod.

"We know you bought high-grade. Where's the smelter?"

Harry tried to shake his head loose from the man's grasp, but he was not talking.

Fender pulled his gun and looked at Hall.

"No," said Hall. "Not yet. Get a knife."

One of the men came back from the kitchen with a butcher knife.

"Peel him, but don't kill him," said Hall.

Harry struggled, then grew calm.

"I'll tell," he said.

Hall looked up at the ceiling to see it shaking and swaying, and for a moment, this strange action did not register. The coal-oil lamp swung crazily on its wire, causing shadows to dance on the canvas walls of the saloon.

"What the hell," said Hall.

Some of the men moved toward the entrance, and one looked outside. A man on horseback had a rope looped to the ridgepole and was spurring his horse to pull the tent down.

"Hey, you!" yelled the man.

He leveled his gun just as the ridgepole gave way and the tent came down on the men inside. The horse and rider disappeared at the sound of the gun.

The lamp broke as it fell, and flames spurted up from the coal-oil-soaked sawdust. The men tried to hold the canvas up with one hand and shield their faces and stamp at the fire, but smoke drove them out.

Fender dragged Harry behind him, and they all stood outside and watched the canvas saloon go up in bright flames.

"Somebody get after that rider," said Hall. "Fender, take Stiles up to the mine."

The men scattered to get fresh horses, and Hall walked along slowly behind Fender, who half-dragged, half-carried Harry Stiles up the hill.

Johnny rode hard down the main street and slid off at the edge of town. The horse, crazed with fear from the gunshot and flames behind him, kept running. Johnny ran crouched to the creek bed, scrambled down the bank, and headed back toward the saloon. When he got even with the saloon, he peeked over the edge of the bank and saw flames. The dry canvas blazed brightly, and men came running to see the excitement. Bottles popped in the heat, a box of shells went off, and men ducked and laughed. It was a good show.

Johnny cussed under his breath. They would not leave until the fire had burned itself out, and then they would be poking through the ashes to see what could be salvaged. In the meantime, Harry would talk or the others would double back and find him. Either way, time was running out.

Johnny ran back down the ravine until he was behind the Golden Ram saloon. The tent was dark, shut down for the night, and Johnny crept over the bank. He eased up to the back of the Golden Ram and touched off a match. The canvas caught, and Johnny ran back to the stream and jumped over the bank. He lit running and hurried upstream in time to see the men at Stiles's notice the fire at the Golden Ram.

They ran as a mob down to the Ram. That was one fire they wanted to put out before the whole town went up.

Johnny waited a few seconds, then crept over the bank. The fire at Stiles's place was out, but the light of the fire at the Golden Ram spread almost back to where Johnny stood. Nothing remained of Stiles's saloon but a few smoldering planks and barrels and the wood stove in the kitchen. Johnny approached the stove and tested it with a finger. The stove was too hot to handle. He stooped and put his shoulder to it, but the heat burned right through his shirt. Johnny ripped off his bandanna, wrapped his hands in it, and took hold of the stove. He could feel the flesh burn, but he lifted. The stove stuck. Johnny got a better grip. He sweated to swing the stove before some curious man happened by to see him.

The stove moved an inch, and Johnny heaved. The stove swung sideways, revealing the trap door. He threw the trap door up, but the steps leading down were dark.

"Toomey?" said Johnny.

He took a step down and came in contact with something hard—a gun barrel.

"It's Johnny," he said. "Let's get the hell out of here!"

Gantzel turned back to the others behind him in the cellar.

"It's Johnny," he said.

Johnny crowded past Gantzel and hurried down the steps. It was pitch black in the cellar.

"Toomey?" said Johnny.

"Right here."

"We've got one minute to get out."

"What's happening?" asked Pejack.

"No time to talk," said Johnny. "They'll be back soon."

"Each of you carry an ingot," said Pejack.

"Head for the creek," said Johnny.

He crossed to the Kearnses.

"You all right?" asked Johnny.

"Yes," said Cleo. "Are you taking us?"

"I don't see any reason now," said Johnny.

"They're going," said Pejack.

"We've got to run for it," said Johnny. "She'll hold us back."

"She's going," said Gantzel.

Johnny felt a gun in his back.

"Move that before I wrap it over your head," said Johnny.

"She goes," said Goodhard.

"Take them out, Goodhard," said Pejack.

Goodhard herded the Kearnses up the stairs.

"No time to argue, Johnny," said Toomey. "Let's go."

They crowded to the top of the steps, the men carrying the gold, and Pejack took a quick look, then darted across the open ground and dropped out of sight into the creek bed.

Goodhard took the Kearnses next, then Toomey and Bianco made it safely.

"You first," said Gantzel.

Johnny crossed open ground, and he could see the miners silhouetted against the flames of the Ram. Nobody was looking back in their direction.

When Gantzel was safely in the creek bed, Pejack pointed upstream and led the way. They went splashing up the shallow creek out of the circle of light, the men bowed under the weight of the gold, the girl slipping on the uneven footing. Owen put his arm out and steadied her, but his eyes were on the cut bank, looking for a low spot where he could get. It was just possible he might be able to make a run for it and get away in the dark. But then he thought of Cleo, and he could not stand to leave her with these men. And he made his choice.

16

Brooks Hall came up out of the cellar beneath what was once Harry Stiles's Saloon. He carried a lantern, and many of the hundred men waiting for him at the top of the stairs carried torches.

Brooks stood for a moment regarding the mob.

"I'll give a thousand dollars for each man caught," he announced.

A low wave of sound escaped the mouths of the mob.

"Five thousand dollars for Orville Pejack," said Brooks Hall. "Five thousand for Johnny Terrell. Dead or alive."

The men started to move.

"Wait!" shouted Fender.

They held.

"Don't wipe out their tracks."

He pushed through the mob, carrying a lantern, and led the way to the riverbank. The footprints of the thieves were plainly visible. It took only a few minutes to be sure which way they had gone.

"Upstream," said Fender.

"Spread out," ordered Hall. "Find where they left the creek."

The mob moved quietly along both sides of the creek, scouring the uneven earth, stooping to study the ground under torchlight.

"Here!" shouted a miner.

They rushed to the spot and saw trampled earth, still wet with tracks, where the gang had left the creek.

"Just minutes ahead of us," said Fender.

"Fan out," said Hall.

The mob spread out and began the climb uphill. The light of their torches and lanterns flickered and danced in the night wind, casting eerie shadows on the scrub brush and broken earth. The trail led toward the boulder field, a natural fortress and hiding place, and the mob grew wary. They advanced slowly, half expecting to be fired at.

Johnny could see them coming. He hurried over the rocks and whispered down into a dark crevice.

"Here they come," said Johnny.

Goodhard and Gantzel were packing the gold on two mules hidden there for that very purpose.

"Bianco," said Pejack. "Take the others and head out. We'll follow. Gantzel, you and Johnny, and I'll hold them off."

Bianco motioned to Owen and Cleo to follow and crept out of the hiding place. Toomey brought up the rear. Goodhard finished, tested the straps, and then led the mules out after Bianco, while Pejack and Gantzel climbed to where Johnny waited.

They sat on the high boulders watching the torches make way up the hillside.

"Afoot," said Pejack. "Good."

Johnny studied the terrain and then turned to look uphill.

"If we fire and fall back to the north, they'll figure we're cutting toward the pass," he said. "We can double back later."

"Fire high," said Pejack.

He leveled a rifle, and Gantzel drew his revolver.

Fender saw flashes of light on the rocks above before they heard the report, and he knew it was muzzle fire. Bullets whined over their heads, and men dropped and hugged the earth.

"Put out those lights," ordered Hall.

A few men returned the fire while others stamped out torches.

"Save your fire," said Fender.

He walked to Hall.

"Can't see to hit them in the boulder field," he said. "Shall we move in?"

Hall looked around at his men, most of them still pinned down.

"That'll take time," said Hall, "and they'll move out in the dark. Bring up horses and send some men up above the field."

The flash of guns came again, and men ducked as bullets ricocheted off of rocks and whined into space.

"North," said Fender, "toward the pass."

"Is it covered?"

"Ten men up there. They'll walk into a trap if they go north."

"Get the horses. We'll drive them ahead of us," said Hall.

Johnny, Pejack, and Gantzel caught up with Toomey first. He was straggling behind the others, one hand holding his side.

"What's wrong?" asked Johnny.

"I'm all right," said Toomey.

The others went ahead as Johnny walked beside Toomey.

"That kick in the kidneys?" asked Johnny.

"That's it."

"Here," said Johnny.

Johnny put an arm around Toomey and held him, and together they stumbled and ran over the uneven ground to catch up.

"The girl is too slow," complained Goodhard.

"Put her on a mule," said Pejack.

Gantzel grabbed at Cleo, but she stepped back.

"I'll get up by myself," she said.

"Come on, girlie," said Gantzel.

Owen stepped between them, but Gantzel pushed him back as if he were nothing and grabbed Cleo. He lifted her up on a mule's back and laughed at her, and they went on, faster now to keep up with Bianco.

Owen walked beside the mule to steady his bride, and she looked down at him.

"I tried," he said.

"It's all right. He didn't hurt me."

"I'll kill him," said Owen.

"Don't do anything foolish."

But Owen did not hear her.

It was dawn by the time Brooks Hall and Fender led the mounted men to the base of the cliffs. Brooks looked up at the insurmountable wall of granite, and Mick shook his head.

"They couldn't," said Fender. "It isn't possible."

"Then you tell me where they went," said Brooks.

Fender did not say anything. He knew it had been done somehow, and it was best to keep quiet.

"Away clean," said Brooks. "They got away clean. Well, let's start fresh. Find where they went up."

The men rode along the base of the cliff, staring up at the towering walls. It appeared useless. No one had ever been known to scale the cliffs.

"If there's a way the Indians would know it," said Fender.

"There's an old Ute living up in the meadows," said a cowboy.

"Go get him," said Hall.

He got down and sat on a rock and lit a cigar,

and Fender slid down and stood before him.

"You're not going on today, are you?" asked Fender.

"Why not?"

"These men haven't slept for two days."

"Neither has Pejack or Johnny Terrell. Are you too tired?"

"No. I'm ready."

"You'd better be," said Hall. "You're in trouble, Mick."

"How's that?"

"If we don't get them inside a week, it'll be you who decorates the tipple. Understand?"

Mick understood.

"They're heading for Mexico," he said. "I'll send someone back to telegraph ahead."

"Have ammunition, food, and warm clothes brought up here, too. This may be a long ride," said Hall. "And Mick, bring plenty of rope."

Bianco sat singing softly to himself by the fire. Johnny roasted venison on green sticks, while Gantzel cleaned his handgun, and the others just rested. The gold was stacked prominently in view of everybody, and the mules were picketed in the grass close by. Gantzel stayed near the gold as if it were his. Cleo slept close to Owen, who held her enclosed in one arm. Toomey lay awake, the pain in the small of his back too fierce to let him sleep.

They ate venison with their fingers, and Gantzel went to relieve Goodhard on watch, and after Goodhard had eaten, he leaned back and stretched luxuriously. His eyes fell on the gold, and he smiled, and then he looked at the girl. She did not see him looking.

"We'll sleep for an hour and move out," said Pejack.

"What's the hurry?" said Goodhard.

"We're not clear yet," said Pejack.

"They'll never get over the cliff," said Goodhard. "Not the way we came. Why kill ourselves?"

"You can rest in Mexico," said Pejack.

"What about them?" said Goodhard, indicating the woman and her man.

"What do you mean?"

"We don't need him," said Goodhard.

"If you've got any ideas, forget them," said Pejack.

Goodhard looked around the fireplace at the faces of the others, but he got no encouragement. Pejack waited, but Goodhard did not press it, and they all settled down to sleep.

Pejack let his eyes close, but he listened, and he opened his eyes at every little stirring. Toomey got some fitful rest, but once, when he got up and walked away to make water, he hurt, and there was blood. He cursed silently. He was rich at last, but a thoughtless kick by a sadistic cowboy had ruined him, and he was a very old man.

Johnny did not sleep. He put the rifle close by and lay with his back to the fire and watched the stars change in the night sky.

Goodhard thought about the woman and went to sleep smiling. Bianco slept like a child.

They were ready to move before dawn. They shivered in the cold, improperly dressed for the altitude, without provisions, and there was a nip in the air.

Goodhard and Gantzel packed the gold, not letting anyone else touch it, and they led the mules out after Bianco, their heads close together in talk.

"What I wouldn't give for a hot cup of coffee," said Toomey.

"How do you feel?" asked Johnny.

"Fine."

Toomey did not look good. His ruddy complexion had turned gray.

"Johnny," said Pejack, "you watch the Kearnses."

"Why me?"

"You want to see them make it. They're all yours."

"Let Toomey ride one of the mules," said Johnny.

"What's wrong with him?"

"He's sick."

"I'm not," said Toomey.

Pejack looked at Toomey.

"Go ahead if you want to," said Pejack.

"I'll walk like the rest," said Toomey stubbornly. "Those mules can only carry so much."

Pejack and Toomey went ahead, and Johnny motioned for the Kearnses to lead him out. They walked ahead, and after a while, Owen turned to Johnny.

"Those two men with the mules are plotting," he said.

"I know that," said Johnny.

"What are you going to do?"

"Nothing."

"They'll kill us all. They want the gold, and they want Cleo."

"You worry about Cleo," said Johnny. "I'll worry about the rest of it."

The wind freshened, bringing with it the threat of snow. They were traveling at eight thousand feet, where storms could be expected any time in that season. The sun came up behind solid haze in the east, and when Johnny looked west, he could see a white, angry wall of weather moving toward them. He hurried ahead to Pejack and pointed west, and Pejack saw the storm.

He shook his head angrily, and Johnny took his arm and made him stop.

"What do you want me to do about it?" said Pejack.

"We've got to find cover."

"Where? There's nothing out here."

Johnny left him and walked ahead to catch up with Bianco.

"Hold up," said Johnny.

"I saw the snow. It's bad, a blizzard," said Bianco.

"Where can we go?"

"There is a log cabin ahead, an old one built by trappers years ago. We can make it if we hurry."

They struggled on, whipping the mules, and the snow began to fall. By the time they reached the cabin, they were white with crystals, and the ground was beginning to hold the snow and turn white too.

The cabin was windowless, and there was no door, only a gaping hole that let the wind in. Johnny stayed behind outside to gather wood while there was still time, and when he came in, Bianco had already started a small fire.

A part of the sod roof had caved in, and Johnny went out again and cut pine boughs to cover the hole. There was nothing to do about the door. It had been closed with a stretched deerhide tacked onto a frame, but the hide had rotted and been eaten away by animals.

It was warm enough in the shelter if they stayed close to the fire, and the walls cut the wind. Pejack stood at the doorway watching the snowflakes grow larger and fall thicker until they became a solid wall. He could not see twenty yards, and it was high noon.

He hit his fist against the wall.

"When will it end? We can't stay here," he said.

"It's best," said Bianco.

"Nobody's going to follow in this," said Gantzel. "The snow will cover our trail. Relax."

He looked at Cleo.

"Want to get out of those wet clothes?" he asked.

Cleo was shivering against Owen, and she did not move.

"We're all right," said Owen.

"I wasn't talking to you," said Gantzel.

"I bet I could keep her warm," said Goodhard. "Come here, baby."

"Leave her alone," said Johnny.

Goodhard and Gantzel exchanged glances, then Goodhard stood up and took a step toward Cleo.

Johnny's rifle came up, and Goodhard stopped. Johnny swung the rifle to cover Gantzel, who was reaching for his pistol.

"Go ahead," invited Johnny.

Gantzel let his hand fall back.

"Pejack," said Johnny. "When a man makes me a promise, I expect him to keep it."

"Leave her alone," said Pejack. "Haven't we got enough trouble. Go check those mules, Goodhard."

"Why me?"

“They’re your job. If we lose them, I’ll make a pack horse out of you.”

“Do you think you can?” asked Goodhard.

Pejack just looked away from him, and after a moment, Goodhard turned and went outside into the storm.

17

Hall and Mick Fender huddled against a boulder. They were heavily coated, and Fender had a blanket over his head and held it out to protect a small, smoldering fire. It was hard to keep the fire going. Other men crouched by trees and rocks around other fires.

"Want to turn back?" asked Fender.

"Can't. The summit will be under two, three feet of snow," said Hall. "They'll be tied down too. We'll push on as soon as it lets up. We'll pick up their trail easy in the snow."

"It could last all day," said Fender.

"Not this time of year. Storms blow over easy this time of year."

But it did not blow over.

By afternoon, a group of men came to Hall and asked him to turn back while they could still get over the pass.

"Go back if you want," said Hall. "I'm staying. I'll give every man that stays with me an extra hundred dollars."

"You'll run out of food, or if the storm keeps up, you'll die out here," said one. "Either way, it's no good."

"There's nothing but Indians between here and the border," said another.

"Go back if you want, but I don't want to see any of you that quits still in Lucky when I get there."

Most left, and when they had ridden away in the snow, Hall could count only Mick and five others. Even the old Ute Indian had turned back.

"Can't blame them," said Mick. "Well, we don't need more than seven. A hundred men are unwieldy and noisy to handle."

"I'm not going to lose the Lucky," said Hall grimly. "I'd get them if it was only me on their trail."

"Will you lose the mine if we don't get the gold?"

"Yes, I'd lose it, but that isn't going to happen."

Gantzel and Goodhard had the gold stacked on their side of the small room and they did not leave it alone. One of them was always beside it.

Johnny noticed that first one then the other had gone to speak in undertones with Pejack.

"Plotting," said Toomey.

Johnny nodded in agreement.

"I can almost tell what they're saying," said Toomey. " 'Why split with so many? A third is better than a sixth. Let me have the woman and I'll give up a portion of my share.' Greedy-gut Goodhard would give all of his gold for the woman or a bottle right now, and let tomorrow take care of itself."

"What makes gold so valuable?" asked Johnny. "The way they've been bringing it out of the ground these last few years should make it common as dirt."

"Gold won't ever be common," said Toomey. "If you found a mountain of gold, it wouldn't be common. You can use it for things like no other metal. It can be beaten to a thickness of two hundred-thousandths of an inch. It's unaffected by heat, air, or moisture, and ordinary solvents. One ounce can be drawn into a wire sixty miles long. Besides, it's beautiful. It has a luster. It's like a superb woman. Women are plentiful, but good ones are rare, and they'll always find a market. Same with gold."

He doubled up and gritted his teeth against the pain, and when he relaxed again, Johnny laid him back against the wall and tried to make him comfortable.

"Thanks," said Toomey.

Johnny went to Pejack.

"Toomey's sick," said Johnny.

"I've been noticing."

"I'd better try for some game," said Johnny, looking into the storm.

"You won't find nothin' out there."

"Depends on where I look. If this keeps up, we'll need food."

"Go ahead," said Pejack.

"I won't be long," said Johnny.

He held Pejack's eyes for a moment, and Pejack knew what was on Johnny's mind.

"She'll be all right," said Pejack.

Johnny pulled his hat down and went out, head down, into the snow. The wind was driving the flakes now. Ground swirls flung snow into his eyes.

It grew dark fast, and when Johnny returned, he almost missed the cabin, and, but for the smell of smoke, he would have walked right by. He brought back two rabbits and stood in the doorway, peering inside. His eyes sought out Cleo, and she was where she had been before, next to Owen. Gantzel and Goodhard sneered at him, and he threw the rabbits at their feet.

"Skin 'em out," he told them.

It was either that or go hungry, and Goodhard began skinning the rabbits.

Bianco laughed.

"Shut up, Mex," said Goodhard.

Bianco's eyes narrowed, but Cleo said something to him in Spanish, and he smiled at her and sat back.

It was the first time Cleo had spoken to any of them of her own free will, and now she sat up away from Owen.

"Speak English," Goodhard told her.

"Let me help," said Cleo.

Goodhard looked at her in surprise and nodded, and she crossed to him, and together they got the rabbits skewered on sticks to roast. Owen watched her silently, and Gantzel, too, envy on his face.

"How do you like yours?" she asked Bianco. "Well, medium, or rare?"

"Cooked," he said.

"Gantzel?" she asked.

"Just so you serve it," he told her.

She moved among them easily now, out of her shell at last. The only one she did not speak to was Johnny.

The snow did not let up, but it was warm and friendly in the cabin. The rabbits made no more than a bite or two for everybody, but it was like a feast after the events of the last two days.

"Sit here," invited Gantzel.

"No, here," said Bianco.

Cleo looked from one to another. She did not look at Owen.

"Are you married, Mr. Gantzel?" she asked.

"Not so's you'd notice," he said.

"Bianco?"

"Sure, two times, maybe more. I can't remember."

"Cleo!" said Owen.

She sat down beside Bianco.

"Cleo," said Owen again, but his voice was plaintive this time.

"What are you up to?" said Pejack.

"Nothing," said Cleo.

"Go sit with your husband."

"Leave her be," said Bianco.

She got up suddenly to avoid his encircling arm and sat down by Gantzel.

"That's better," said Gantzel.

He tried to put his arm about her, but she took it firmly and placed it by his side.

"How about me?" said Goodhard.

"You're too fat," she told him.

Everybody laughed.

Cleo stood up again and sat down by Owen.

"I'm tired," she told him.

He held her close, and she went right to sleep against his chest. The others watched enviously, but Owen closed his eyes and held her tightly.

Johnny leaned back against the wall next to Toomey.

"She'll go with the strongest," said Toomey. "The one who can protect her can have her."

"Do you blame her?" asked Johnny.

"No, but she's already made up her mind," said Toomey. "She was just testing."

"How do you mean?"

"Grandpappy once said to me, 'When a woman is in the company of two men and addresses herself to only one, you can be sure she's busy beneath the table with the other.' "

Johnny thought about it. He and Pejack were the only ones Cleo had not had any truck with.

Bianco came to sit beside them, and they quit

talking. Pejack put wood on the fire and lay down, and after a while they slept as best they could. Johnny awoke suddenly to find Bianco leaning forward. He looked in the direction of Bianco's gaze and saw Goodhard standing over Cleo.

Goodhard was pulling her by the arm, and Cleo was shaking her head, "No." She was resisting him silently, trying not to awaken the others.

Johnny started to move, but Bianco put out a hand. He already had a gun out.

"I will only shake my finger at him," whispered Bianco.

And he pulled the trigger.

The roar of the revolver was deafening. Goodhard let go of Cleo and somersaulted backward from the impact of the slug.

Pejack and Gantzel jumped to their feet, guns drawn, but Bianco covered them.

"It can go off again," he said.

Gantzel and Pejack crouched down and turned Goodhard over.

"Right through the heart," said Pejack.

"He was after Cleo," said Johnny.

"Kind of a final way to stop it," said Gantzel.

"He was warned, *verdad*?" said Bianco.

He blew the smoke from the barrel of his gun and holstered it, pulled the hat down over his eyes, and lay back against the wall.

Gantzel pulled the corpse over next to the wall and left it there. They all settled down once more, and Bianco smiled up at Johnny from under the brim of his hat.

"We'll help each other," he told Johnny. "*Verdad*?"

"Sure."

"That Goodhard, he was a pig."

Johnny did not say anything. He was thinking that Bianco was as hard a man as he had ever met.

The snow stopped at midnight, leaving more than a foot of white on the ground. The moon came out, and the world was blue, cold, and beautiful.

"We can travel now," said Pejack.

Johnny looked at Toomey's face, and Toomey tried to smile.

"For a man of sixty who's spent twenty years of his life in bed, I should look more rested," said Toomey.

"You can't travel," said Johnny.

"I can't afford not to," said Toomey.

"Bianco," said Johnny. "Where's the nearest town?"

"Forty, fifty miles south," said Bianco.

"I'll take you there," Johnny told Toomey.

Toomey shook his head, "No."

"To hell with the gold," said Johnny.

"Son, I'm a miner," said Toomey.

He struggled to his feet, and Johnny helped him. He tried to take a step, faltered, and caught himself.

"Give it up," said Johnny.

"If I die I'll die rich," said Toomey. "Help me get to the mules."

Gantzel, Pejack, and Bianco loaded the gold onto the mules and watched silently as Johnny helped Toomey climb on the lead mule. It was only a question of time before there was one less to share with, but they did not like to see Toomey on the mule.

Bianco went first, and Johnny led the mules. Pejack came next, and Gantzel brought up the rear behind Owen and Cleo.

Owen leaned down to Cleo.

"What were you up to?" he whispered.

"Nothing."

"The way you act, you're just egging them on. I can't help you if you egg them on."

"You can't help anyway," she told him. "I'm sorry, Owen, I didn't mean it like it sounds. Forgive me for whatever happens."

"You talk as if we're through."

She shrugged.

"Don't quit on me," he told her. "I'll think of something."

"Please don't," she pleaded. "You'll only get hurt."

"Cleo," Gantzel called. "Walk with me."

She turned around to smile at him, then dropped back, and they walked together.

"What are you going to do when we split up?" he asked.

"I don't know. Go back to Santa Fe."

"Why?"

"It's home."

"That's not for you. You won't stay with Kearns long either."

"Say it out loud," she told him. "Don't beat about the bush."

"Come with me to Mexico City."

"With you and your gold? How long would it last?"

"Long enough."

"No, I don't want a few weeks or months with any man."

"What do you want?"

"More than you have. A man who can make money, not spend it."

"There's enough in this train to last a lifetime."

"It would take a good man to get it," she told him.

"The man who did it would be man enough for you?"

"Even I would be afraid of a man like that, I couldn't resist him."

"You're not suckering me into getting shot, are you?"

"You're the one who brought it up," she said,

and she patted his face and walked ahead to Owen once more.

Toomey fell off the mule, and Johnny tied him back on, and they struggled ahead. The mules broke trail, making it easier for those behind, but everybody was cold through, and they strode along swinging their arms and clapping their hands to keep warm.

Johnny looked back to see blood trickling from Toomey's mouth. He called to Bianco to stop and then started to untie Toomey.

"What's wrong?" said Pejack.

"He's hemorrhaging," said Johnny.

Pejack looked forward to where Bianco waited, then back along the trail in obvious nervousness.

"I'll give him ten minutes," said Pejack.

"What good will that do?" asked Johnny.

"A half-hour, a day, it doesn't matter," said Pejack. "He's ruptured something inside. He's bleeding to death."

Johnny put Toomey down on the snow and stripped off his own coat to pillow the old man's head.

Toomey coughed, opened his eyes, and looked around. He saw Cleo walking ahead to Bianco and heard words exchanged and the pleasant laughter of a woman's voice on the still air.

"Woman will be the last animal civilized by man," said Toomey. He coughed blood again and was silent.

"You never had a grandpappy, did you?" asked Johnny.

"No," said Toomey. "I made him up like I did everything else."

"You made up them sayings yourself," guessed Johnny.

"I read them in a book. Johnny, I'm scared."

"I'll take care of you," he told the old man.

Johnny looked up to find Cleo and Bianco standing over him.

"Why don't you make a travois?" said Cleo. "Then he could lie flat. He wouldn't bounce as much."

Johnny went right to work cutting supple aspen trees. He tied his coat to two limbs and secured the travois Indian-fashion behind the lead mule. They laid Toomey on the bed of the travois, tied him down, and started out again.

Bianco seemed to know the way, and as it grew lighter, he stepped up the pace. Pejack glanced over his shoulder from time to time, but the hills were heavily wooded, and he could not have seen anybody following. Cleo and Owen were hard-pressed to keep up, and Gantzel began prodding Owen, egging him on to go faster.

"I'm going as fast as Cleo can walk," complained Owen.

"Then you'd better get her to take bigger steps," said Pejack. "If she gets to be a burden, I won't wait for her."

"You think Bianco or Gantzel would let you leave me behind now?" asked Cleo.

"They'll do as I say."

"Will they?" asked Cleo.

And Pejack knew she was right. If it came to a showdown, he was no longer top man.

18

Fender entered the cabin cautiously, his gun ready, while the others hung back in a semicircle around the cabin. Fender was inside for not more than a moment, then he came out, holstering his handgun.

"One dead inside," he told Hall.

"Know him?"

"Goodhard, the foreman at the corrals. The ashes are almost cold in the fireplace. That means they're hours ahead of us."

"But traveling slow from the looks of their trail," said Hall. "Two mules, five men, and a girl. We'll make up time. Let's go."

They climbed into their saddles, and Fender led them out at a good clip. They stopped once more where the others had made a travois for Toomey, and they saw fresh blood on the ground.

"Somebody's hurt," said Fender. "He's been riding a mule. That makes it six men and the girl."

"Fighting among themselves already," said Hall.

"Which makes our job easier."

"I don't want them to make it easier," said Hall. "I want the pleasure myself."

They rode again, harder now, their horses'

hoofs throwing up snow, thundering down the plainly marked trail between trees, ducking to avoid branches.

As the sun rose higher, snow fell from branches, releasing the pine boughs to whip in the air, and snow plopped to earth. The men sweated inside their heavy coats. Their faces were preoccupied, tense with excitement, as they closed on their goal.

Toomey coughed hard, uncontrollably, and blood ran out of the corner of his mouth. Johnny wiped away the blood and sat helplessly by. The others stood away from them, trying not to see. They were looking up high where Bianco hung on to a limb of a tall pine, scanning the wilderness. For some time, they had realized he had been leading them first one way, then another. He was lost. He could not find the way with snow on the ground, and he had finally climbed the tallest tree he could find to see if he could recognize a landmark.

But now Bianco was looking intently back toward the summit. Blue jays rose up on brilliant wings along the back trail. He heard jays caw loudly far away, and he swung down quickly, scrambling to earth.

"What is it?" asked Pejack.

"Here they come," said Bianco.

"How many?"

"Can't tell. Too far off."

Pejack started to move toward the mules.

"What are you doing?" asked Gantzel.

"Let's go," urged Pejack.

"No good," said Bianco. "We can't outrun them."

He and Gantzel were studying the terrain. A short distance ahead, the ground dipped out of sight, then rose again.

"There?" asked Gantzel.

"It will have to do," said Bianco.

"What are you talking about?" asked Pejack.

"We'll have to stand and fight," said Gantzel.

"There may be a hundred of them," argued Pejack.

Bianco ignored him.

"They're coming hard," he said to Gantzel. "Maybe we can ambush them. Two of us here, two ahead in the trees on that rise of ground."

"Good," said Gantzel. "But who takes the mules?"

"Whoever goes ahead," said Bianco. "I'll lead the mules on to bait the trap."

"Pejack and I'll go ahead," contradicted Gantzel. "You and Johnny stay here."

"You and I'll go on," corrected Bianco.

"No time to argue," said Johnny.

He stood up and looked at Bianco and Gantzel.

"Take the mules and go easy," he told them. "Pejack and I'll stay here. Just see to it you don't spill Toomey. He's worse, and I want to find him alive. Understand?"

"Cleo," said Bianco. "Go."

He pointed ahead, and Cleo and Owen started, and then he led one of the mules while Gantzel pulled the other, and the four of them went down the slope out of sight and a moment later reappeared climbing the other side.

"You're crazy," said Pejack. "They'll keep on going."

"Bianco knows we have to beat Hall first," said Johnny. "Pick a tree and start climbing. Wait until Hall gets down into that depression, then open up. We'll have them in our crossfire."

They each ran to a tree and swung up into the lower limbs. Johnny climbed until he had a view of the bottom of the hill, then checked the action of his rifle to make sure it was not frozen. He could hear the sound of hoofbeats as he got extra rounds out of his pocket. Bianco and the others were out of sight now, and Johnny hoped Hall and his men would come on hard, falling into the trap.

The noise of horses grew louder. They were coming on the run, and Johnny peeked around the trunk of the pine. Down below on the ground, he could see one rider, then another, and behind them more, barreling in at a dead run. Johnny leaned back against the trunk of the tree and raised the rifle, getting his sights set.

Fender was on the lead horse with Hall right behind, and the others strung out at intervals of a few yards.

As Fender came into the clearing beneath the trees, he could look ahead and see the trail plainly. It led down a slope, and he could see sign as the trail went up the opposite side again, disappearing into the trees. He did not miss the signs of the stop but figured they had rested here, and he spurred his horse, the rowels causing the animal to leap ahead.

The riders piled down the slope. Johnny could hear leather squeak and horses snort and suck air. He raised his rifle again and took dead aim at the last horseman.

The first shot and the second came before Hall knew they were in the trap, then two more shots came from directly ahead, and Fender fell out of the saddle. Brooks Hall heard a bullet whistle past his head, and he reined back hard, pulling his horse up on its hind feet. The next shot caught the horse in the chest, and when it came down again, it folded up and fell, and Hall rolled out of the saddle. He kept rolling, clawing for his gun.

Three men and one horse were down, the riderless horses ran whinnying and stampeding in the snow.

Mick Fender got drunkenly to his feet, dragging at his gun, but another bullet from the trees ahead knocked him backward, and he lay still.

Brooks Hall grabbed for the stirrup of a runaway horse, but it pulled free from his grasp, and he lay stretched out in the snow. A close bullet threw snow in his face, and he realized he was being shot at from behind, too, and he jumped to his feet and tried to run.

The marksmen in the trees threw rapid crossfire at the posse. Another man went down, his horse dragging him, when a foot caught in the stirrup. Riders scattered both ways up and down the gully, several escaping, one more falling backward out of the saddle at the last moment, and then the crossfire switched back to Brooks Hall, scrambling aimlessly for cover where there was none on the floor of the gully.

Hall was hit once. He staggered sideways and threw up his hands. His eyes were wide with a plea to live.

Johnny lowered his gun and turned his head away.

Bullets poured into Hall. He spun this way and that from the force of the slugs as he fell, hit half a dozen times.

It was all over except for the sound of horses thrashing off through the underbrush, and Johnny hung on to the tree for a moment, then started climbing down.

"Get those horses," yelled Pejack, scrambling down.

Johnny walked down into the gully and cautiously turned over the bodies of men. They were all dead.

"Never mind them," said Pejack. "Help me catch the horses."

"Go to hell," said Johnny.

Pejack stood looking down at Brooks Hall's riddled body. It was not a pleasant sight, but Pejack smiled, then he turned on his heel and ran to catch one of the runaway horses. Johnny climbed the ridge and found Bianco waiting.

"Where's Gantzel?"

"Gone to make sure the Kearnses don't wander off. How many got away?"

"A couple."

"But that's Brooks Hall down there?" said Bianco, pointing.

Johnny nodded.

They rounded up the loose horses, four of them, and Johnny made a fire, while Gantzel brought the mules and the Kearnses in. It had turned colder. Johnny knelt by Toomey and found the old man still breathing, and he unstrapped him and got him by the fire. Toomey's eyes were open but sightless.

"He's got to have something to eat," said Johnny.

Cleo brought coffee and bacon that she found on one of the horses and helped him cook. The posse had been prepared for a long march.

There was extra ammunition in the saddle bags, a coffee pot, tin plates, cups, and sourdough to make bread, and there were even extra blankets, canteens of water, and tobacco.

They had their first good meal in days, and it helped revive them.

Johnny hand-fed Toomey, but it did not seem to bring him around. Gantzel watched Johnny baby the old man narrowly.

"We've got to think about moving on," said Pejack. "How far until we get out of the mountains, Bianco?"

"Long way. Three hundred miles to the plains, where it's warmer."

"Looks like it could snow again," said Pejack.

"We can make it now that we've got horses," said Gantzel.

"Just four horses," said Bianco. "Six to ride and Toomey."

"There's two we could leave behind," said Gantzel.

"Who?" asked Pejack.

"Don't say it," said Johnny, looking around at Gantzel.

"But there's three hundred miles of broken country ahead, mostly mountains, before we're safe from snow," said Gantzel. "We can make it on the horses, but it's almost impossible if we have to go so slow carrying him along."

"You can double up on the horses," said

Johnny. "Toomey's sticking with the gold. That's what he wants."

"How do you know?" asked Gantzel. "He can't even talk anymore."

"It's settled," said Pejack. "We'll ride double and switch off, and we'll keep Toomey. He earned his share."

They put out the fire and traveled, pulling Toomey on the travois behind a mule. Cleo rode double behind Bianco, and Owen behind Johnny, and when the horses tired, Cleo got on behind Gantzel, and Owen behind Pejack.

They stopped before dark to make camp, and Johnny made a broth for Toomey out of a squirrel he had shot along the way. He kept Toomey warm and as comfortable as possible, and the miner seemed stronger by morning. He did not speak, but he seemed to know Johnny, and he smiled.

The little caravan wound its way slowly down out of the range of mountains, and they could see a flat, arid valley ahead and another range of mountains ahead. Owen was riding behind Johnny.

"Do we have to cross those mountains?" asked Owen.

"Yep, and a couple others, too," said Johnny. "It's a long way to Mexico."

"Aren't there any towns between here and there?"

"Bianco's seeing we don't come close to any."

"If you could get Toomey to a doctor, he might pull through."

"I know it."

"Why don't you try? You could get away with it. Maybe you could take Cleo and me, too."

"Toomey doesn't want it that way."

"For God's sake, why not?"

"He wants to stay with the gold."

"It'll kill him."

"He knows that, but if I took him to a town and he pulled through but lost his share of the gold, he'd just as well be dead. That's the way it is."

"They'll probably cheat him out of it anyway, even if he lives."

"Most probably."

"I thought I could talk to you," said Owen angrily. "I thought you were the one civilized man in the bunch. You're just as bad as the rest."

"Maybe you'd better ride with Pejack for a while," said Johnny.

Owen slipped off the horse and strode to Pejack, who had been watching. He gave Kearns a hand up, and they went on. Gantzel was leading the mules, and he made a turn around a weathered stump on the steep hillside. The mule got by too closely, and the travois caught the stump and tipped over, and the mule plodded on, dragging Toomey upside down.

Johnny raced to Gantzel and jerked the lead rope out of his hand. He jumped down, stopped the mule, and got the travois turned back over. Toomey was scratched a little but not hurt badly, but Johnny glared at Gantzel.

"Watch where you're going," he told Gantzel.

Gantzel rolled his eyes back in his head in disgust and turned to Pejack.

"This will take forever. I could walk to Mexico faster," Gantzel complained.

"If you dump him again, you won't get to Mexico," said Johnny.

Gantzel reined his horse around and faced Johnny so as to be ready.

"Try me," said Gantzel.

He spat the words out.

"Stop it," said Pejack.

"Let him take care of the old man," said Gantzel. "I won't no more."

"That's fine," said Johnny.

"You take care of him," Pejack told Johnny.

"But he can't use the mule," said Gantzel. "Not with the gold. Let him pull the sled behind his horse."

Bianco had been listening.

"We are going too slowly," he said now. "Give Toomey and Johnny their share and leave them behind."

"No," said Pejack.

"We have too far to go," said Bianco.

"We'll go together," said Pejack.

"Why?" asked Gantzel.

"They'd get caught," said Pejack. "What would they do with a seventy-five-pound ingot, trade it over a saloon bar? In Mexico, we can get it smelted down. There are men who'll buy it and keep their mouths shut. Besides, how would we divide it evenly now? There's no way to cut up a bar."

"We should be traveling thirty or more miles a day," said Gantzel. "We can't do twenty with him along."

They all looked at Toomey, who lay pale and silent on his stretcher. The whiskers of his chin were a white stubble, and his sightless eyes gave him a moronic, pitiful appearance. He did not look like he could live another day. They all showed the results of their experience. The men were bearded and dirty and hollow-eyed, and Cleo was as ragged and tired as the men.

"We'll camp tonight and make a decision in the morning," said Pejack. "A rest will do us good. Maybe we'll think of something come morning."

19

Cleo and Owen lay together by the fire under a blanket, the others ranged around them. Gantzel snored, and Pejack turned restlessly in sleep.

Owen waited until the fire died down, and then he put a hand on Cleo's shoulder. He touched his mouth to her ear.

"Cleo?" he whispered.

She nodded to let him know she was awake.

"I'm going to get away tonight."

She shook her head violently, "No."

"We've got to. There's not much more time. Once we get out on that plain below, there'll be no place to hide."

"It's too dangerous," she whispered. "Wait till we get to Mexico."

"I'll never make it," he said, but there was no self-pity in his voice. "I'm not kidding myself. They'll keep you alive, but they don't want me. I've got to try now."

"Johnny won't let them touch you."

"He's one against three. He'll turn his back once, and Bianco will stick a knife in him."

"Johnny can take care of himself."

"Are you going with me or not?"

"We'd both die out here in this wilderness. You don't know how to get along. Even if they didn't catch us, we'd die of starvation."

"That's better than letting them kill me like a sitting duck. I'll take my chances. I just want to know about you. If we stay, you'll end up with one or all of them. What do you say?"

"Owen, I'm no lily. I've been with men for money, why wouldn't I sleep with one to save my life?"

"It's different now. You married me."

She was silent for a moment, wanting to believe it, but he knew the answer before she spoke.

"I haven't changed enough," said Cleo sadly.

"Then you won't go?"

"No."

"You would if it were Johnny Terrell asking," he accused. "You'd believe he could escape."

"Don't be ugly," she said. "You'd do better to stay and take your chances. There's a tough streak in you that's good."

"I'm leaving as soon as the fire dies out," he told her grimly. "Don't try and talk me into staying."

The men slept restlessly on the hard ground. Only Toomey was silent. Pejack got up once, went into the woods, and then came back and put another piece of wood on the fire. Owen waited. He was tense with waiting. Gantzel snored beside the stack of gold bars, his fingertips resting lightly against the nearest one.

When the fire died out at last, Owen laid the blanket back carefully. Cleo clutched at him, but he pulled free and got to his knees. He ran softly toward the staked-out horses, not making a sound, and Cleo held her breath. Kearns was hardly out of sight before Bianco got up, glanced at Cleo, then walked in the direction Owen had gone.

"Bianco," said Cleo softly.

He stopped.

"I'm cold," said Cleo.

Bianco looked from her to the blackness where Owen had disappeared.

"He's just gone to relieve himself," she said. "Put another log on the fire."

"No, *señora*," said Bianco.

He walked purposefully after Owen and Cleo jumped up.

Johnny awakened, and so did Gantzel and Pejack.

"What's wrong?" asked Johnny.

"Bianco's after Owen," said Cleo.

"Where?" asked Johnny.

She pointed into the darkness, and they heard a horse whinny.

Johnny got up and started after Bianco.

"Stay here," he told Gantzel over his shoulder.

They waited, staring into the black. The stars were bright overhead, and the air was still, but they could not hear anything until Bianco and Johnny came back, marching Owen before them.

"He was after a horse," said Bianco.

"Running away?" asked Gantzel, elaborately. "Bad boy."

He took a step forward and hit Owen in the face. Owen fell back, but Johnny kept him from falling.

"Let me finish him," said Gantzel.

"Wait," said Pejack. "Was he really taking a horse?"

"It is the truth," said Bianco. "And she knew it."

They all looked at Cleo.

"That's all I've been waiting for," said Gantzel. "Let's get rid of him. It's bad enough having to nurse Toomey, but not being able to sleep for fear Kearns is going to steal the horses is too much."

"She knew it too," said Johnny. "She'd have let him get away. Aren't you going to finish her, too?"

Gantzel glared at Johnny.

"What are you protecting them for? What's she to you? I'll kill him. I'm not afraid to do it," said Gantzel.

"Nobody's going to be killed," said Pejack.

"You shut up," shouted Gantzel. "I'm tired of hearing you. You're an old lady, Pejack. I'm sick of you."

Pejack did not react rightly, and Gantzel knew he had Pejack cowed.

"Wait," said Bianco.

"Whose side're you on?" asked Gantzel.

"Don't be hard with me," warned Bianco. "I won't hold still for you."

Gantzel faltered. He had beaten one of them, but he did not want to press his luck, and Bianco was a better man than Gantzel.

"How do you stand?" asked Gantzel more reasonably.

"Kearns is dangerous," said Bianco. "But we are four against him. We can handle one man."

"And the girl?" asked Gantzel. "She was letting him get away. It's time we did something about her."

"What do you have in mind?" asked Bianco.

"Separate them," said Gantzel. "We can tie Kearns to a tree at night."

"And the woman?" asked Bianco.

"She can share our blankets with us," said Gantzel.

"None of that," put in Pejack.

"Stay out of it," Gantzel told him. "I've waited long enough."

"Who chooses?" asked Bianco. "Us or the girl?"

"She ain't got a choice."

"Take turns?" said Bianco.

"Why not?" said Gantzel.

They both looked at Cleo, and she stared at the ground.

"You don't have to," said Johnny to her.

Johnny stood away from Owen and faced Bianco and Gantzel. Pejack moved away from all of them. If Johnny had counted on help from Pejack, he was disappointed.

"Why fight among ourselves?" asked Bianco. "You can have your turn."

"I don't want it," said Johnny.

"Somebody's got to watch her," said Gantzel. "She'll turn her husband loose in the night."

"She tried to fool me," said Bianco.

"You can tie her up, too," said Johnny.

"Maybe she doesn't care," guessed Gantzel. "Tell him, Cleo, or you might see Terrell and Kearns dead on the ground here."

"You don't have to," Johnny told her again, but his eyes never left Bianco and Gantzel.

"It doesn't matter," said Cleo hopelessly. "I'll sleep with any of you."

"It's settled," said Bianco.

"How do we decide?" asked Gantzel.

"Tomorrow," said Pejack. "It's almost dawn. Let's get going."

It was true. The eastern sky was whitening, and it was close to dawn. Johnny stood fast until Bianco and Gantzel turned away, and he watched Cleo start to build up the fire to get breakfast.

Johnny went to take the horses to water, and Owen sat down disconsolately beside Toomey. He looked at the old man and was surprised to see him awake and bright-eyed.

"I was watching," said Toomey, his voice husky.

"I'm sorry you had to see my shame," said Owen.

"Shame? She's a brave woman."

"Brave like a wild thing, not much like a lady."

"Yes, she's a wild one. Never been tamed. That's why I like her."

"You sound like an intelligent man," said Owen. "How can you admire the uncivilized?"

"Look at it this way. My grandpappy used to tell me that the wilderness of nature has no need to be anxious about its reputation. So it is with Cleo."

"But Gantzel and Bianco? They're wild, too. Do you admire them?"

"There's a difference. They're not really free of fear. Take Bianco. He's cunning and dangerous, I'll admit, but cunning is only a cover for incapacity."

"I never thought of it like that. It makes him less fearful."

"That's why I said it, but don't underestimate the man. Now I'm tired."

"Sorry," said Owen, and he got up. "Can I get you something?"

"Hot coffee. I can smell it boiling, and I never smelled anything so good in my life."

Owen went to the fire.

"Toomey's better," he told Cleo.

She looked up at him, and he smiled at her.

"Don't look so worried," he told her. "It won't happen. I won't let it happen."

Johnny came back and found Toomey sitting up, drinking coffee, and he sat down with him.

"Decided to come back to life, I see," said Johnny. "I knew you wouldn't let me have your share."

"Gold? I'd almost forgotten it."

"I'll bet."

"I witnessed the little ceremony."

"Good bunch, isn't it?"

"I've seen worse."

Toomey broke off with a violent coughing fit, and when he was done, he looked terribly pale and weak.

"I can still get you to a doctor," suggested Johnny.

"No use now. Kidneys are ruptured. I can help you, though."

"How?"

"The two of us could take them."

"Don't get any ideas. You'll only make it worse."

"Kearns isn't going to let his wife go to them. He loves her, and there's good stuff in him. Her, too."

"I know."

"They'll have to get both of you before they can have her. Pejack will side with them to save his skin. Let me help."

"I'll work it out," said Johnny. "You just get well. This is my fight."

"Why have you stuck?" asked Toomey. "You never wanted the gold."

"I just had the idea you needed someone to look after you."

"An idea? You've got a lot of ideas. Some of them concern what's right and wrong."

"Maybe."

"Remember, son, in a war of ideas it's the people, not ideas, that get killed."

20

The column of horses and mules wound down the mountain to the hot floor of the valley, but it was not hard going until they were on the level. Dust boiled up behind the horses, and Toomey coughed long and hard. Johnny and Pejack stopped and got down. They washed the old man's face with cool water and let him rest on his travois while Gantzel and Bianco, with the Kearnses riding double behind them, sat waiting impatiently ahead.

Toomey held his hand up to his face and found an ant crawling on a finger. He looked at Pejack.

"Men aren't much," said Toomey. "Even ants can run a complex community without the sweet use of reason."

"What are you trying to say?" asked Pejack.

"Think about it," said Toomey. "Johnny and the Kearnses need you on their side. You're a strong man, or you were once. What happened to you?"

"I don't know," said Pejack.

"You help them," Toomey told him.

Pejack looked at Toomey, but Toomey folded his hands over his breast and closed his eyes before Pejack could speak.

"I'm tired," said Toomey.

Pejack looked at Johnny, a worried expression on his face.

Johnny felt for a pulse and then undid Toomey's shirt and felt for a heartbeat, but Toomey was dead.

"Come on!" shouted Gantzel. "We can't wait all day."

Johnny began untying the straps that held Toomey to the travois.

The others rode back slowly and sat looking down curiously.

"He's dead," Pejack told them.

"What are you going to do?" asked Bianco.

"Bury him," said Johnny.

"Leave him," said Gantzel. "Now we can make time."

Johnny went on about his business.

"Let him bury the man," said Pejack. "We can noon here while it's done."

Gantzel hesitated, then swung down and put up his arms for Cleo. She slid down into Gantzel's arms, and he set her lightly on the ground.

They made dry camp while Johnny scooped out a shallow grave and put Toomey in it. Johnny piled a layer of flat rocks on the body to protect it from animals and smoothed dirt over them to hide the grave from Indians. It took a long time, working alone, and when he walked back to where the others sat, he found Gantzel mauling Cleo. Gantzel was trying to fondle her and kiss her while the others sat silently by. Owen looked on grimly while Cleo fended Gantzel off in silence, not crying out or making noise. She was suddenly as strong as a man and very determined.

Bianco was playing with his knife and watching Owen, keeping him pinned down. Pejack had his back to the scene.

"What's going on?" said Johnny harshly.

Gantzel did not stop.

"He won," said Bianco. "We flipped, and he won. You weren't here."

"That's enough," said Johnny.

Gantzel whirled around, and Bianco got slowly to his feet.

"It's all over," Johnny told them.

"You don't say," hissed Gantzel.

Cleo crawled away from Gantzel and lay on the ground, her shoulders shaking.

"I knew we'd have to settle," said Gantzel. "How do you want it? Hot lead or Bianco's knife. He's better with the throwing knife than most men are with a gun."

"Pejack!" said Johnny. "Choose!"

"I can't, Johnny," said Pejack.

"Then stay out of it," Johnny told him.

"Why do you do this?" asked Bianco. "We're all rich men here. What does the girl matter? Why die now?"

"I just came along for the ride," said Johnny.

"I don't want the gold. Now that Toomey's dead, there's no use going on."

"Then take a horse and leave," said Gantzel. "Take Kearns with you."

His voice was changed, not as hard. He was ready to deal, and he licked his lips, and Johnny decided he would go for Bianco first. Underneath, Gantzel was scared.

"I want Owen, Cleo, and the gold," said Johnny. "And four horses."

Bianco laughed.

"You're wrong," Gantzel told Bianco. "He's going to give the gold back. He doesn't want it for himself!"

He said it in disbelief.

Bianco stopped laughing, and his face settled into an awful composure, eyes dead and body completely relaxed.

"Take it," said Bianco.

Bianco's hand rose to indicate the mules packing the gold, and the gesture hung in the air for all to see for what seemed an eternity, and then Bianco and Johnny went for their guns.

Johnny was first. He held the Henry rifle in his right hand, and he raised the barrel and pulled the trigger with one slick movement. He did not miss.

Bianco's gun was already out, and it went off, but Bianco was falling backward, and the bullet split the sky.

Gantzel was very fast. He slapped leather, and the gun came up. Owen dived across the open ground toward Gantzel, and the gunman changed targets. Johnny was still levering a second shell into the chamber of the rifle, and Gantzel took a chance and gave his first shot to Owen.

Owen Kearns was slammed to earth by the force of the heavy bullet. He never reached Gantzel.

Gantzel and Johnny shot a second time, simultaneously, but Johnny had taken more time to aim. The bullet hit Gantzel in the mouth and came out the back of his head, carrying his hat and half of his skull with it. He was dead on his feet and fell where he had stood.

Johnny whirled on Pejack, levering the Henry, but Pejack had made a run for it. He was up on a horse, and he shot his gun in the air, stampeding the other horses and the mules, still packed with gold.

"Pejack!" yelled Johnny.

Pejack snapped off a shot at Johnny, and Johnny ducked to his knees while Pejack spurred his horse. The horse took off after the mules, and Johnny raised the rifle.

"Pejack!" shouted Johnny once more.

But Pejack rode on wildly, his body flattened against the horse's neck to make a small target.

Johnny put his cheek down on the stock and sighted.

Cleo heard the explosion of the rifle and a split second later a scream, and then Johnny was beside her. She looked up and saw Pejack lying flat on the sand and the mules grazing peacefully where they had stopped. She let Johnny lift her up, and they went to Owen.

"He's breathing," she said.

She put her husband's bloody head in her lap while Johnny examined the wound.

"Creased the skull," said Johnny.

"Badly?" she asked.

"Probable concussion."

"Will he be all right?"

"Better let him lie quietly till he comes around. May not be able to travel right off."

They washed and dressed the wound, and she sat with Owen while Johnny rounded up the mules and horses. He took off the saddles and bridles and unpacked the mules, and he disposed of the bodies of the dead before he joined Cleo.

"He hasn't stirred," she said.

Johnny felt the man's pulse and then put a hand on his forehead.

"Pulse is weak, and he's running a fever," said Johnny. "Keep him warm."

Cleo bundled Owen in blankets and went to stand with Johnny. She regarded the gold and then Johnny.

“What if he doesn’t pull through?” she asked. “Are you really going to return it?”

Johnny looked at the gold.

“That’s the cause of all our trouble,” he told her. “Didn’t you learn anything?”

“Yes.”

“What?”

“He’s a better man than I gave him credit for.”

“Then stick by him.”

“I intend to. That doesn’t keep me from wondering what it would have been like if things had worked out differently for us.”

He shrugged, and they turned together and returned to Owen. Johnny made a fire, and Cleo fixed supper. It turned cold when the sun was gone, and Johnny got a blanket.

“I’m tired,” he said. “Think I’ll turn in.”

He walked away from her and spread his blanket out of the circle of light.

It was dark and still when Johnny woke up suddenly. Cleo was kneeling beside him, and she was shivering, and he reached out and put a hand on her cold arm.

“Is Owen all right?” asked Johnny.

“Yes,” she said. “It’s me. I’m cold, and I can’t sleep.”

He pulled the cover aside, and she crawled in and curled up against him. They put their arms around each other, and after a while, Johnny felt her grow warm, and she relaxed, and then she slept, and that is how they said goodbye. When she woke up in the morning, he was gone, leaving a map showing which way to go.

21

A posse out of Arizona Territory found them, the man and the girl on horseback, leading two mules carrying over two hundred thousand dollars in gold bullion.

They had a tale to tell, of being held hostage by bandits for almost a week in the godforsaken wilderness of the Colorado Plateau, an area as big as a nation and most of it never seen by the eyes of white men.

The bandits had fallen to quarreling over the girl and the gold and killed each other off, or else they'd never have lived to tell it and bring the gold out safely.

The man wore a dirty bandage on a badly infected wound, and the girl was done in, but she was still a beautiful thing for all the dirt and cracked lips and sun-parched skin from the desert sun.

"You say they're all dead?" asked the deputy U.S. marshal in charge.

"Every last one," answered the man. "Almost got me, too."

The marshal re-dressed the man's wound while he questioned them, and at last, one of the cowboys turned to Cleo.

"Say, ain't you Cleo Esteban out of Santa Fe?" he asked.

"I'm Mrs. Owen Kearns," said Cleo.

"I'd bet you were Cleo Esteban."

"You heard the lady," said Owen, his voice flat and hard.

The cowboy dropped it. He wasn't about to argue with a man who could live through a gunfight single-handedly between a whole pack of outlaws.

The girl smiled at her husband, and they envied the man.

And that was that.

About the Author

Peter Dawson is the nom de plume used by Jonathan Hurff Glidden. He was born in Kewanee, Illinois, and graduated from the University of Illinois with a degree in English literature. In his career as a Western writer, he published sixteen Western novels and wrote over 120 Western short stories for the magazine market. From the beginning, he was a dedicated craftsman whose stories are noted for their adept plotting, interesting and well-developed characters, their authentically researched historical backgrounds, and his stylistic flair. During the Second World War, Glidden served with the U.S. Strategic and Tactical Air Force in the United Kingdom. Later in 1950, he served for a time as Assistant to Chief of Station in Germany.

After the war, his novels were frequently serialized in *The Saturday Evening Post*. No less gifted as a master of the short novel and short story, his fiction has retained its classic stature among readers of all generations. One of his finest techniques was his ability, after the fashion of Dickens and Tolstoy, to tell his stories via a series of dramatic vignettes that focus on a wide assortment of different characters, all tending to develop their own lives, situations, and predicaments, while at the same time propelling the general plot of the story toward a suspenseful conclusion.

Center Point Large Print
600 Brooks Road / PO Box 1
Thorndike, ME 04986-0001 USA

(207) 568-3717

US & Canada:
1 800 929-9108
www.centerpointlargeprint.com